The Slender Man

Dexter Morgenstern

Artwork by Anna Stockbring

1: The Sabbath

I can't say I'm a spiritual person, but I definitely enjoy the Sabbath. My family is Jewish, and every weekend we get together with the Hawthorns to celebrate. We used to go to a synagogue, but ever since we moved here to Murphy, North Carolina, we've been celebrating the Sabbath the traditional way, at home. The closest synagogue here is two hours away and not good enough to be worth the trip, so every week we alternate houses with the Hawthorns, our best friends, to celebrate. To tell the truth, they are our only true friends out here. Shana, their oldest daughter is like my sister. Every Sabbath we take turns sleeping over at each other's house.

I met her on my first day at school here when we moved, and was so happy that I wasn't the only

Jewish person there, because honestly this town is so under-populated for its size that I've met at least half of the people here. Shana has an olive complexion; a button nose that she complains is too big, long thick black hair, and beautiful brown eyes. She's almost exactly my size and even our birthdays are in the same month, May. Ever since we found that out we always celebrate our birthdays together and even ask for the same presents. When we turned fourteen, we both got our own guitars. When we turned fifteen, we both got Labret lip rings. We're not sure what we want this year. We will both be turning sixteen so we want it to be something special, but a car would be too much to ask of our parents.

It took us forever to learn how to play our guitars well and even now she's still having trouble plucking. I'm a natural at it. We found that she is a much better singer though so mostly I play the more difficult notes on my acoustic guitar, and she plays single chords while focusing on singing. It works out well, but both of us are terrible at writing lyrics and guitar tabs so often we just practice our favorite songs.

Right now we are singing the prayer Adon Olam. We always play it, because it is my seven-year-old brother Adam's favorite hymn- well, actually his favorite song in the whole world. I'll admit that we're a little unorthodox with the way we

The Slender Man

conduct our Sabbath. Normally a song like Adon Olam would be played at the end of a Rabbi's sermon just before the food, but we don't follow that anymore. Instead we play a whole bunch of songs for our family's entertainment, and then we eat. Her sister Denise likes the song "Complicated" by Avril Lavigne, so we will do that next.

As we play I look around the room at our audience. They're all sitting at the dining room table, eyes on us. My family, the Redwoods, is sitting to our left. Adam looks very happy and is mouthing the words while we sing. Next to him sits my mother Sarah. She has shoulder length brown hair that's starting to gray (after all, she's turning forty-five soon), and hazel eyes that look just like mine except... older. Mom doesn't seem too impressed by our sometimes off-key playing. Sometimes Shana's guitar chords and mine don't mix well, or sometimes we'll sing on two very different notes making it sound weird, but she still looks happy that we're playing. Next to her sits my dad and he looks just as happy as ever. You can almost see tears of joy in his eyes through his almost rimless glasses. He is balding on the top of his head but is still very proud of the thick bushes around it. So proud in fact that he dyes it black to make himself look younger (although he isn't pulling it off), and just covers his bald spot with his dark blue yarmulke. I modify my hair too though.

I'm a natural brunette like my mom, but I think blonde looks better on me, so I bleach mine. Most people are shocked when they find out it's not naturally blonde. Next to him is my grandmother Hannah, but I call her Bubbe. My grandmother is very old and always seems melancholy, but whenever someone speaks to her she always smiles and appears to be enjoying herself. I don't know, maybe it's just her ashen hair and many wrinkles that make her appear so grim. Despite being in her eighties, she's not senile at all, but I think that has to do with the fact that she has lived with us instead of being thrown into a nursing home.

On the other side of the dining table sits Shana's family, the Hawthorns. Her father Matt Hawthorn is fully bald but that doesn't stop him from having a good time. He's a joyous man that's putting on some weight, but doesn't even seem to care. By contrast, his wife Barbara is very slim. She has short black hair and very few wrinkles on her face. Most people don't believe she's over forty. Shana's sister seems to be taking up her father's eating habits as she is a little too big for a seven year old, but her curly brown pigtails fashioned by her sister make the mix look cute.

We finish the prayer and our families applaud us. Shana and I take each other's hand and give a low bow as a single unit before playing our next and last song for Denise. I let Shana sing this one alone

The Slender Man

while I play guitar. We found that only one guitar is necessary and well, I'm not so good at singing this one either. We play it a little differently than the original version. Shana starts with the first verse and when she finishes I come in slowly with the guitar.

After that song we have a little more applause but then we set our guitars down and join our families at the table.

Our moms get up and run into the kitchen to fetch the challah bread and the meal.

"Alyssa?" asks Mr. Hawthorn. "

Yes?" I answered.

"Your brother is going on the camping trip to the lake tomorrow right?" he asks.

"Yes, he is," I say, ruffling Adam's hair. He hunches forward. Adam hates when I touch his hair, but it's a habit I picked up when he was a baby and still haven't dropped. "Do you two mind if Denise stays over tonight, too? So she can just be dropped off with Adam? I'd appreciate getting to sleep in for the weekend, and she's got everything she needs in her backpack in the car," he asks. I look at my Dad and he just shrugs.

"Fine with me," he says. I look back at Mr. Hawthorn and smile

"Sounds like fun. She'll get to play with Adam," I answer. He nods his appreciation.

At that, our mothers reentered the room carrying trays. Mrs. Hawthorn sets hers down first and quickly heads back to the kitchen. My Mom sets her tray down and we sing the Motzi before she removes the cloth to reveal two warm loaves of challah- braided bread. While doing this, Mrs. Hawthorn returns with one final tray with nine shot glasses. Seven are full of red wine and two are separated from the rest full of grape juice for Adam and Denise. It's a Jewish custom to enjoy wine at the Sabbath but all our parents agree that children can only have it when they turn thirteen, so the two younger ones have a ways to go. As Mrs. Hawthorn distributes the glasses, she waves one hand to cue the blessing over fruit and the Sabbath. "

Baruch atah Adonai..." I start.

"Elohaynu melech ha'olam," Shana joins followed by the rest of them, until we all finish the prayer with a loud

"L'chayim!" which is toast that means "To Life!"

After we eat the breaded chicken, baked potatoes, and green beans, Barbara and Matt Hawthorn say their goodbyes and then take their leave. Shana and I begin to rush up stairs but my mom stops us.

"Nope, not yet. You need to get these dishes done first," she said. I sigh, but that's the way we do things. Mom cooks, Dad cleans the counters and

The Slender Man

table, I do the dishes, and Adam stays out of the way. It would be more of a chore to wash dishes on the Sabbath because our meals were always special and since there are more people, there are more dishes, but Shana always helps and the job goes by more than twice as fast.

Once we finish the dishes, we head up the wooden staircase to my room. Shana and I both have the habit of using the walls of the stairs for balance instead of the banister. Most of our walls seem too cluttered with portraits and decorations, but everything is at least neatly organized. That is, until we get to my room. Marked by a worn down Karen-O poster on the door, my room is the most cluttered of them all. Almost every inch of wall is taken up by some poster or picture or even some of the drawings I drew when I was Adam's age.

On my floor are various clothes. Clean or dirty? I don't care, and I just kick them all into a pile in the corner on top of my school papers. Oh well, I'll sort through them tomorrow when I start my essay that's not due till Tuesday. I can hear Adam and Denise playing what sounds like an old Dance Dance Revolution game, but with the lack of rhythm in their trampling I bet they aren't getting very high scores.

The clothes are just part of the mess in my room. Even my decorations are placed messily. I have lopsided posters of some of my favorite bands like Chevelle and Paramore. Mom doesn't stress me too much about the cleanliness of my room. She's more worried about my grades. I'm lingering on the low end of a B average and she doesn't want to see it decline any further.

After I clear out a decent space on my floor, I pull out the chair from my desk and move it near my vanity for Shana to sit. I take the vanity stool and Shana and I both proceed to remove our makeup which isn't really much. We both wear eyeliner and lip gloss, and Shana wears a little blush on her cheeks, but when we finish removing the makeup from our faces, we begin reapplying nail polish.

"What colors should we do this week?" I ask. Shana looks at the assortment of colors laying on my vanity and picks out two. We always wear two different colors of nail polish, alternating the colors on every other fingernail.

"How 'bout... green, and black?" she asks.

"Dark green or light?" I respond

"Light," she answers without hesitation.

As we apply the nail polish to our fingernails, we begin to speak. We mostly talk about school. She and I don't really hang out with any of the other students. It's not that we're anti-social or that we don't get along with the other students, it's because both of us have parents that work in the school. Her mother is the school counselor and my father is the vice principal.

"At least having parents at the school keeps the boys respectful," she says.

"Yeah, but when prom time comes that means we will probably be the only ones without a date," I respond. She shook her head.

"Come on Lyss, if they're afraid to approach us because of our parents, don't you think they'd be even more reluctant to reject us?" she suggests.

"That's evil," I laugh.

"How's track?" she asks. I've been part of the track team for the last two years.

"Awful!" I exclaim.

"Leanne has got some kind of problem with me. She always sprints to pass me and then when she's tired she makes a point to body-block me so I can't get ahead."

"Doesn't that slow her down too?" she asks. I shake my head.

"No, she and I are the fastest on the team by like ten seconds, but she finishes just ahead of me like half the time now just because she does that," I explain. I'm getting angry just thinking about it.

"Is it really that hard to pass her?" she asks.

"I don't know. I guess I'll just fake her out and pass her on the opposite side I approach from," I say. She claps once, as an idea just hit her.

"No! I have a better idea. When she speeds up to pass you, you speed up. That way she'll tire out faster and won't be able to keep up with you. She'll probably end up slowing down to third or even worse if she tries too hard," she explains. I like that idea.

"Well hey I'm going on my weekend jog tomorrow morning after I drop my brother- er our siblings off. You wanna come?" I ask. She looks hesitant.

"I mentioned to my mom about our run last time. She doesn't want me going into the forest like that. She's even surprised that your mom lets you do it alone," she says. I bite my lip and fumble my labret ring with my teeth.

"But as long as we don't tell her," she continues. A sly smile crosses my lips. Shana is a worrier though so I can tell that's not the right approach.

"My mom realizes it's dangerous too," I say, standing up.

I look around the mess in my room to find my purse. It's a small colorful Alice in Wonderland bag that I've had since I was ten. It's pretty worn now, but I've always used it. I open it and reach in.

"My mom always has me carry this," I say, pulling out a small blue cylinder.

"Pepper spray?" she asks. I nod.

The Slender Man

"Your momma lets you carry that around?" she asks.

"Makes me," I correct. "Just don't mention it to anyone. It's not really... legal per se," I add.

"Well what's more legal then? A dead girl, or a crook with burning eyes?" she asks. "That's what my mom said!" I exclaim. I clasp both hands to my mouth, thinking I was too loud.

I look at my clock and realize it's only eight. It only seems darker because of the opaque purple curtain that hides my window. My mom buys into the urban legend that people will spy on me undressing if I don't block the view from the window.

"So anyway, if you're trying to outrun Leanne, won't I slow you down on the trail?" she asks.

"Oh no that trail is like what three miles? I can't run that at top speed. I can barely make it at a medium pace," I laugh. The trail is not really a paved trail, but more of a path I found that can take me all the way to the school district and even further, so I can get to almost anywhere important in the town from it.

We spend the rest of the night talking about our schoolwork. The essays we have to write are on creative historical fiction. It's a project that affects both our history and our English grade, so it's kind of important. We both have to make up short stories where we place ourselves in a historical event and then explain how our lives worked through it. Shana brings up the idea that our stories should collide so that it was the same story, but through both of our points of view. I think it's a great idea, but it makes our essays that much harder.

"At least we got plenty of time to do it," she says.

"Yeah, and if I get an A on this my grades will go up, so my mother will stop breathing down my neck," I say. "

So, what subject? The Civil War?" she asks. I shake my head.

"No, Ms. Alder will probably see a dozen of those and get so bored she drops our grades for it. How about something Asian?" I ask. She thinks about that for a second.

"I haven't had Chinese food in a while," she mumbles. From there we continue to sidetrack until it gets late. Not really late for a Saturday, but because of the whole trip tomorrow we won't get to sleep in like normal. So we drop at about ten, with her sleeping on a mat in the floor. I sleep peacefully.

2: The Accident

I brush my teeth. Shana is changing into some of my workout clothes since she didn't bring any of hers. It took us a while to find some in the cluttered mess around my floor, and I had to face-palm myself when I found a full work-out outfit in the closet where they belong. We found a matching Nike vinyl jacket and pants for her to wear. I'm wearing my white and gray hoody and navy blue running shorts. I spit the water into the sink and then rinse my mouth out. I floss too. I know it's something usually done at night, but I always forget and end up flossing in the morning. When I get back into my room, Shana has already brushed her teeth and is putting on some of my sneakers, while the day clothes she brought are placed neatly on my bed so she can find them easily when we get back.

"Alyssa, hurry up!" Adam groans from outside the open door. I hold my palm out at him without even looking. I'm still grumpy from getting up at six rather than noon on a Saturday, so I'm not in any mood to be nagged. Although to be fair, Shana and I did cost him ten minutes while looking for clothes, so he's been waiting for a while. I make sure to grab my keychain, water bottle, and phone and then stuff them into my jacket pocket. It's not a very good phone. You have to flip it open, and it still has a dial pad, not like one of the smartphones, but I broke three cellphones in the past year so finally my parents got me the most durable one they could find. My keychain is pretty empty. It just has my house key and Mace.

After Shana and I are both ready, I inspect Adam. I can see the ties to his swimming trunks hanging from his jeans. He's also wearing flip-flops, a T-Shirt, and a green jacket, but I notice something missing.

"How is Mr. Mario gonna know who you are?" I ask. He thinks for a second before realizing my point.

"Oh yeah," he exclaims, sticking a hand underneath his jacket and pulling out his nametag. "It needs to be visible," I say.

"Where's Denise?" Shana asks. Adam points downstairs and I look to see Denise, fully ready to go, lying against the door half asleep. Glad I'm not the only one still tired. At least my jog will wake me up.

"Do you have your permission slips?" Shana asks. I completely skipped out on that, but luckily Adam is on top of the situation and pulls out a clumsily folded paper with the necessary signatures.

"Alright, let's go," I say, and lead Adam downstairs. Shana rouses Denise, who picks up her backpack and opens the door. As we head outside I fix my hair into a ponytail and take the lead. Luckily we're just on time as I can see the bus pulling up to the stop down the street. Adam and Denise run to the stop, thinking they're gonna miss it, but the driver just pulls up to our driveway.

The bus door opens and I can see Mario Douglas, who everyone calls "Mr. Mario," the kindergarten and elementary school driver that I see every morning as I drop Adam off, with a half awake smile on his face. Mr. Mario is about thirty or so and has a well-trimmed beard. It looks like he has a receding hairline but he covers it with his driver's cap, so you can't really tell. He looks really mean every time I see him. He looks even grumpier now that he's working on a Saturday and his smile doesn't fool me, but Adam says he's really nice and that he brings a bucket of candy for all of the children to take from every Friday afternoon. So maybe the only reason I think he seems mean is because he's not a morning person.

Adam, already out of breath, steps into the bus panting and hands Mr. Mario the permission slip, followed by Denise who didn't run quite as far as Adam did. Mr. Mario looks at me and gives me a wink and a nod before closing the door and driving off.

"That's... creepy," Shana says from behind me when the bus is far down the road.

"What is?" I ask.

"He winked at you. He doesn't even know you," she says.

"Well maybe he's just being nice," I shrug, but even I have my suspicions, though so far he hasn't tried anything so I give him the benefit of the doubt.

"Come on," I say, beckoning Shana to follow me as I take off. I always leave the neighborhood in a slow jog before hitting the tree line. Once we are at the stop sign that marks the three-way intersection before the woods, I stop and do twenty jumping-jacks, and a quick stretch. I don't bother stretching my arms, but I do stretch my legs and hips, and I even throw in some ankle rotations. The woodland path I run on every week isn't necessarily treacherous, but I have tripped a few times on a tree root or sudden slope, so I don't want to twist my ankle by accident.

When we are ready, I run down the street and into the forest, with Shana close behind. I go straight in for about a quarter-mile before I reach a tall tree. The tree isn't at all different from the others, but I recognize it well because it marks my first turn. Around the left of the tree is a slight incline. It seems like a longer stretch than it really is, but that's because my legs always burn going uphill. Once we reach the next flat stretch I make another right and head along a seemingly straight path with the occasional turn that ends up forming a subtle semi-circle at the end, and the end of that circle is my mental mile-and-a-half marker.

"Oh Alyssa!" pants Shana. I turn to see Shana catch up to my side.

"I left my phone at your house... did you bring yours?" she asks.

"Yeah," I answer without even needing to check.

"Okay good," she says. Shana is a little paranoid about trips through the woods or even leaving her house alone, so being without a phone makes her feel even more insecure. We continue along the woodland path that I've traversed at least a hundred times by now.

We reach the halfway point, a small clearing in the woods that leads to an actual paved trail, shaped at a right angle. If we go left on the trail we end up in the school district, a place we don't want to so much as think about until Monday, and the right way leads to a small park. This point means it's time to turn around, because the loop will end up being over three miles. We stop and catch our breath. Shana hunches over from weariness. She does exercise, but she's not so used to running.

"Did you bring any water?" she asks. I pull out the transparent blue water bottle I brought, down half of it, and then hand the rest to Shana, who finishes it off.

While she's drinking I open my phone to look at the time. It's eight after seven in the morning.

"When did Mr. Mario reach our bus stop?" I ask.

"Uh ten till?" she says.

"So then eighteen minutes, give or take. Not so bad," I say.

"Don't you have an actual timer on that thing?" she asks. I shake my head glumly. I run in place, shaking my arms for a few seconds before Shana follows suit. We are about to return the way we came when my phone rings. I answer it. It's my mom and she's speaking so hastily that I can barely hear her.

"Where are you? Why aren't you home!?" she asks, almost frantic.

"We're out jogging, Mom. What's wrong?" I ask, worried.

"You need to come back now!" she shouts.

"What's wrong?" I repeat, getting frustrated.

The Slender Man

"There was an accident. Your father and I can't wait for you. We're going to the hospital in Andrews," she says.

"An accident? With what, the bus?" I ask. "Yes your brother, come home now." "Wait, Mom!" I shout, but she has already hung up.

"What's wrong?" Shana asks.

"There was an accident with my brother. They say they're going to the hospital," I say.

"Oh my god! Is Denise okay?" she asks.

"I don't know she didn't say, but we have to go," I say, taking off. I run back, with Shana right behind me, adrenaline pushing me forward. My memory guides me through, but my mind is going off in all sorts of directions. *Did the bus crash? How badly is he hurt? What if he's dying? What if he's dead now?* I keep thinking to myself. My eyes get watery and my heart races at those thoughts. It seems like much more than eighteen minutes to make the return to my house, but my lack of breath and numbing legs tell me it was much less.

"Alyssa!" I hear. I turn and see Shana way back, just emerging from the woods. She catches up and we run inside. As soon as I'm inside, I hear her phone going off. Shana rushes upstairs past me to answer it. I walk upstairs and wait a few minutes while Shana talks to her mother. She's speaking too quietly for me to hear what she's saying. After the phone call, Shana comes and speaks to me.

"What happened?" I ask.

"The bus went off the road, and crashed into the Valley River" she says, looking at the floor.

"How bad is it?" I ask. She shakes her head.

"They said that some of the kids were killed, and others are hurt, and have been rushed to the hospital," she continues.

I grab her hands and stare into her face.

"Who? Who did they take to the hospital?" I asked fiercely. I'm not just worried for her, but for Adam as well. My parents didn't say whether or not he was okay, just that they were going to the hospital. She looks up at me.

"I don't know, they haven't released names," she answers.

"Well then there's still hope. Denise and Adam could be at the hospital," I say, trying to reassure both her and myself. She looks at me and shakes her head.

"But Denise can't swim," she says softly, and leans forward onto me. I hold her to my chest while she cries. Adam can't swim well either though. We've been to lakes before but he's always been heavily supervised. He wouldn't be able to swim out of a bus. Then again, most parts of the Valley River you can walk through, but if it ran into the deeper section. Or if the bus were on its side letting it fill with water…

The Slender Man

My heart sinks at the thought, but before I give up, my phone rings again.

"Are you home yet?" Mom asks. "Yeah, yeah. What about Adam?" I ask.

"Adam's at the hospital," she says. "Is he okay?" I ask, relieved.

"No, we don't know if he'll make it, but you need to come down here," she says. Shana can hear the conversation too.

"And... Denise?" she asks. "Who is that? Shana?" Mom asks.

"Yes is Denise at the hospital too?" I ask for her.

"We don't know. Her parents haven't arrived yet, and they only told us when we got here that Adam arrived. He's in surgery," she says.

"Surgery? I thought it fell in the water," I say. "The water isn't too deep, so most of the damage was from the crash. Some kids did drown but others were still alive," she explains.

"You need to come. Your brother needs you," Mom continues.

"How do I get there?" I ask. Andrews must be almost twenty minutes away, by car.

"Sheriff Fraser says he's sending someone to pick you two up. Just wait at home," she says.

"Okay Mom," I say, trying to convince myself that Adam will be okay.

"Love you," she says, before hanging up. I put the phone down and release Shana. She lies back against the wall and slumps into a sitting position on the floor, almost unblinking. "Shana, she might be okay. Chances are they were sitting next to each other, and if Adam is still alive then Denise should-"

"Just stop," she interrupts. "I don't want to think about it," she says, her voice melding into a sob. She's hyperventilating and squeezing her eyes shut now, trying to hold back tears. It's clear she isn't convinced that her sister made it, and now she's trying to force the thought out of her head.

"Let's hope for a miracle," I say, more to her than myself.

I go into my room and look at how disheveled I look already. My skin is normally pretty tan from being outside a lot, but the color is drained from my face and I'm a ghostly pale white right now. I can even see residue from my sweat mixing with tears around my eyes

"That cop needs to hurry," I say to myself. The tension is eating away at me and the helplessness, the fact that there's nothing I can do until I get to the hospital gives me a headache. *Maybe I should try Shana's method?* I think. I look around the room, trying to find something to keep my mind on other than the fate of my brother, and find Shana's street clothes lying on my bed. *I should change out of these sweaty clothes,* I think. I fumble around my drawers picking up a blue T-shirt, not even bothering to look and see what image is on it, and some jeans. It would be ideal to shower off before getting into clean clothes, but I don't think I have that kind of time, which is a good thing. After changing (tossing my exercise clothes onto the floor), I take my hair out of the ponytail, and try brushing it. My movements are jittery, making it more difficult than it should be to simply smooth my hair out. I hear a knock on the door which makes me jump. I hurry, grab my shoes and purse, and rush downstairs. Shana is already at the door speaking to the officer there.

"Ms. Redwood?" asks the man grimly when he sees me come down.

"Yes?" I say, approaching him. He's young for a cop, and also pretty scrawny. He has short dirty blonde hair, and his eyes are covered by shades. He's got some cuts on his face, so it looks like he shaved in a hurry today. He sticks his hand out.

"I'm Deputy Yew, call me Terrence. I'm here to take you to your family," he introduces. I shake his hand and nod, not sure what to say but

"Thank you."

"Follow me ladies," he says, and Shana and I get into the back of his police cruiser. I put my shoes on during the ride and slowly tie the laces. I almost don't have the energy to rise back up, until

Shana reaches for my hand and I sit back up, letting her rest her head on me. Deputy Yew doesn't speak much during the ride, but I can tell he's speeding, rushing us to the hospital, so it must be that he's focusing on the road. I look over at Shana, staring absentmindedly at the back of the front seat, and can tell she's still taking the news worse than I am.

"It'll be okay," I say, hoping I'm not lying.

3: The Hospital

The minute hand hits twelve, causing the small hand to move up just another notch. It's nine in the morning now. The accident happened around two hours ago, and I've been waiting in the hospital with no news other than the fact that Adam is one of the survivors. He is one of four people recovered alive from the scene. The other three are Shana's sister, the driver Mr. Mario, and a boy named Kenny Larch. All of them were badly injured and are being taken care of, but the doctors don't appear too certain that they'll all make it. I look around the room. We are in an alcove in the hallway just outside the intensive care ward. The families that the bad news was given to are outside or have gone already. The hospital staff gave us chairs from the cafeteria to sit in while we wait.

To my left is my family, all looking just as worried as me. On the other side of the hall is Shana's family, and next to them are the Larch's. Jason Larch, their oldest son, goes to our school. He's a year older than me, but still in my grade, and he's pretty big for his age. No one really likes him though. I won't say he's a bully, but he's very rude to everyone. He is half white, half Hispanic, but he pretends he's fully Hispanic. He has a badly shaped half-grown moustache that he refuses to shave even though it won't grow enough to form a full one.

He is leaning against the wall with his arms crossed over the long red sports jersey that I don't think he ever takes off, and some black cut-off shorts. He's staring at the ground angrily, and looks like the slightest tick will set him off. His father Martin is standing next to him, but with a more worried look than angry, unlike his son, and next to him is his wife Rita. Despite all of the people in the hallway, the room is very quiet, and I can actually faintly hear the wall clock ticking.

I hear voices coming from the intensive care ward and my eyes lighten up as one of the doctors emerges. He's speaking with Sheriff Fraser.

"...So there were no other parties involved in the crash? He just ran off the side of the road?" asks the sheriff.

"Sir, I really don't know, all I can say is that he doesn't appear to be under the influence of any drugs or alcohol. We'll be able to tell you more when he wakes up, but for now we have to see to the other patients," says the doctor before turning and reentering the ward.

Sheriff Fraser stands in the doorway, hands on his belt, staring at the ground as if he is thinking about something. Is he looking for a culprit? Someone he can arrest? The sheriff is a little overweight, and has thinning black hair. His khaki uniform pants are wet at the bottom, so he must have actually gone to the crash site. "Did they say who's responsible?" asks Rita Larch. The sheriff shakes his head, "Looks like Douglas just ran off the bridge. Might have swerved to avoid a deer or something," answers the sheriff in his deep voice.

You'd think by his voice he'd have a moustache or beard, but he's cleanly shaven, unlike all of the other men in the room. It seems that the sheriff is the only person that looks fully kempt aside from the water on his pants. Mom is still in her pajamas and it even looks like Dad just threw on yesterday's clothes, and it's a similar situation with the Hawthorns.

"So arrest him. He was driving irresponsibly! He doesn't deserve medical treatment!" says Rita. She's known for causing ruckus's over little things, so I can only imagine the kind of hell she'll raise over this.

"Ma'am I can't do that," says the sheriff, raising his hand as if to calm her.

"Then what good are you? You arrest my son for 'loitering', but you won't even arrest the man who killed a dozen children?" she yells. "Ma'am I'm here to get the facts. I need to make sure that there was no hit and run-"

"Of course there was no hit and run! He doesn't know how to steer a bus. He's too dumb to-"

"Ma'am, don't interrupt me. Douglas has been a bus driver here for eight-"

"Don't interrupt my mom!" roars Jason, as he angrily approaches the sheriff. The sheriff may be out-of-shape, but he's way over six feet tall, and puts even taller kids like Jason to shame, so it's weird to see the threatening gaze Jason's giving him.

Deputy Yew steps in and interrupts the bickering to speak to the sheriff. I can't hear what they are saying, but I half suspect that his goal is to pull the sheriff out of that sticky situation rather than inform him of anything important. When the scene is over, I look back at the clock. Only another seven minutes has passed. I look at the ground, wondering how long the surgery will take when I hear footsteps and see a shadow approach. I look back up and see a female doctor with her face mask pulled down to her chin. She has a certain subtle smile that can only mean one thing, and I lighten up when I see it.

"Redwood family? I'm Doctor Spruce," she introduces.

"Our son? Is he okay?" Mom asks.

"He lost a lot of blood in the crash, got a lot of water in his lungs, and his left arm is broken, but he's stable. We're going to have to keep him for a couple days, but it looks like he'll make it," explains the doctor.

It takes a second for the news to sink into my parents, so Bubbe is the first to stand up and thank her graciously. I follow suit, but I'm so happy to hear that he's okay that I give her a tight hug before saying "Thank you." I feel tears in my eyes, and can tell the tears have been waiting, ready to hear about the loss of my brother, but now they are spilling out as tears of joy. My parents are sharing their appreciation when the perfect family is there to ruin the moment.

"Hello? Kenny? What about him?" snaps Jason. Doctor Spruce looks around to face Jason. She is hesitant to answer him, because you can tell she's ready to snap back. "We are still working on the others," she finally says.

"Then chop-chop, let's go!" demands Jason, clapping his hands together fiercely. I catch a look from Shana that I understand instantly. It means *"Why do his parents let him act like that?"* Shana's family is in the same position as the Larch's, but you don't see them snapping and yelling. Dr. Spruce looks like she's about to slap him when a nurse with a little blood on his scrubs, rushes out and makes eye contact with her, shaking his head and pointing his thumb back into the ward.

I can't translate the message he gave her like the way I do with Shana, but I know it means bad news for someone. Both of them rush into the intensive care ward without a word. I look at Shana and see that same look of dread renew in her gaze. She might not have the relief I just received. We wait another five, ten, fifteen minutes? It's too long to want to keep count. Eventually, a lone doctor comes out of the ward, with a grim look across his face. This must be *Dr. Bad News*.

"Hawthorn family?" he asks, looking over at the Hawthorns. They all look at him, but don't say a word.

"Would you come with me please?" he says. They all rise and follow him, not to the intensive care ward, but down the hall. A pit falls into my stomach. There's no use pretending that the worst didn't happen. No self-respecting doctor would lead a family on like that just to say *"She's okay!"* at the end.

The nurse from earlier comes through, with a look on his face equally as grim as the doctor. He turns and looks at the Larches, but he doesn't get to say a word before they realize what happened. Jason steps out and looks at the ground. The parents both hold each other. The nurse stops, realizing that they already know what happened.

"I'm sorry. We tried our best, and it looked like he was going to make it but-"

"The driver? Did he die too?" asks Rita. The doctor opens his mouth as if to answer, but then hesitates. I know what he's thinking: *The driver's okay, but that's not news to tell people like the Larch's.*

"I'm sorry, but we can't release confidential information like that to anyone but relatives and police," he says. Jason looks up from the ground and glares at him. He may be idiotic, but he's not totally oblivious to the facts. He shoves the doctor and rushes into the ward. I jump to my feet. He's going to try and hurt Mr. Mario! Both of his parents rush in behind him, but I'm not sure if they're going to stop Jason, help him, or just watch.

I hear loud footsteps and see both the sheriff and Deputy Yew rushing down the hall to stop him. I take a step forward as if to help, but what am I going to do against a guy like Jason that the police can't? I hear shouting and yells of surprise and objects breaking and slamming. There's a serious fight going on in there. Before I can figure out just how much damage Jason is doing I see Shana approaching. Her eyes are wide open, and before I can even think about what to say I rush over and hug her. She muffles her sobs in my jacket, and I can feel the warmth of her tears against my neck. I think of a million things I can say to try to make her feel better, but I don't want to belittle the justifiable grief she is wracked by. I can't find anything to say but

"I'm sorry." It comes out in a choke and I have to try multiple times to successfully force it out. I try to think of something else to say that wouldn't be redundant, but nothing comes to mind, and honestly, if it was the other way around, I don't think anything Shana could say would dull the pain. Words can't cure this kind of loss. Her parents remain down the hall.

I'm still hugging Shana when the door bursts open. I completely blocked out the noise the Larch's were making. Jason has a bloody nose and is cuffed, being pushed by Deputy Yew who can barely contain him.

"Help! Police brutality! Police brutality!" shouts Rita, but not one of us believes her.

"He doesn't deserve to live while my brother dies!" shouts Jason. I can hear Martin trying to reason with the sheriff, who's walking out behind them with a paper towel against his lip. Jason must have hit the sheriff.

After they all clear out of the hallway, I turn my attention to see my parent's reactions, but they're gone. Bubbe is the only one still there, and she's standing with a look of disapproval across her face. I hear footsteps back toward the other end of the hall and see my parents walking back with the rest of the Hawthorns, attempting to console them as well. They sit down across from us, and Shana and I walk over to sit down next to them. All of us are speechless for over an hour until Dr. Spruce steps out of the ward and looks at us.

"Excuse me? Redwoods?" she asks. We all look at her.

"You can see your son now."

It almost feels like a sucker punch to leave the mourning Hawthorns to go see my brother, but I have to see him for myself. The doctor leads us down the care ward that almost looks no different from the public areas except for the fact that these floors were tiled linoleum instead of carpeted. She leads us around several turns until we get to the recovery ward. We're taken to a room with four beds. Two of them have curtains pulled to hide the patient inside.

"Adam is over here," says the doctor, pulling the curtain on the bed closest to the door.

I almost can't believe my eyes. There lies my brother Adam, who I had inspected this morning before his trip, not four hours ago. He was happy and grumpy, and ready to go have fun. Now he barely looks alive. If not for the oxygen mask on his face, I would doubt he's even breathing. I walk over and reach for his hand. His left arm is in a cast, and this one has an IV attached to it. His hand feels cold in mine. I sit on the edge of the bed. I lean in and kiss him on the forehead. As I do I can see a tear splash onto his face and I wipe my eyes against my sleeve. I stroke his face with my hand gently, and quietly, almost whisper the first couple lines of Adon Olam, his favorite hymn. I sing it slowly and out of melody, hoping he can still hear me. While doing so I can feel more tears coming and move my face away to keep them from falling on him.

I look behind me and see my parents and grandmother keeping their distance, waiting their turn. I get off the bed and let them approach. I slink back into a nearby chair and watch them. My grandmother joins me, but we don't say a word. Mom sits on the bed next to him, where I was, and Dad leans against the wall. Nurses walk into the room occasionally to check on Adam, and the other patient, who I bet is Mr. Mario.

Soon the relief of seeing Adam still alive fades and I begin to worry about Shana. Is she still outside? I look for a clock, and since I don't see one, I pull out my phone. It's one in the afternoon. Have we really been here that long?. There's no way they waited this long for us after hearing the news about their daughter. I may not have lost Adam, but I've lost Denise. That loss is even greater for Shana, but

The Slender Man

I feel that she needs some time alone right now. I see how badly Jason Larch is taking it, and he's taking it out on the people around him, so I can only imagine how terrible Shana must feel, leaving those emotions inside, and they are just two of the families that lost children in that crash.

I slouch back into the chair, not wanting to get up. I close my eyes. *How could something like this happen?* So many children dying at once and all from a small community like Murphy, where almost every resident has personally met at least one of the deceased children. I hear the sound of wind rushing, and open my eyes.

I'm still in the hospital chair, but I can't move. My brain tells my body to move, but I only get a nudge in response. My body is tingling all over, like static is passing through me. Did I doze off? This must be a dream. I try to look around as best as I can with my limited mobility. The room is significantly darker. I close my eyes again, but the wind gets louder, and is accompanied by the sound of screeching static. It matches the stiffness in my body. It's like the static is howling, and it gets louder as my eyes close. *What's going on? Is this a nightmare?* I realize that the howling static seems to be coming from my right and I move my eyes in that direction.

Then I see it. Just out of the corner of my eye stands a dark figure, but I'm not sure what it is. It's shadowy, and its movements are violent and jagged, like static, but I can only see it through my peripheral vision. *Why couldn't this happen with my face turned to the right?* I realize that it's standing over Adam's bed, and I open my mouth to say something, but nothing comes out but wind, nothing but an exhale. I try harder, but still nothing. I keep trying, watching the blackness. I start trying to yell, and then I scream, and although I fail in doing so, I can hear my voice, just a little squeak. I push my voice out as hard as I can and can hear a slight moan. I get some feeling return and keep trying. My voice gets louder and louder until I feel a jab on my wrist.

"Alyssa!" I open my eyes.

"Are you alright?" asks Dad. I look around. I'm still in the hospital. I look and see three confused pairs of eyes on me, but the room is bright with afternoon light and clear of dark beings. Adam's heart is still beating.

"Oh... um yeah, it was uh. Just a nightmare," I say as my thoughts return to me.

"Sounded terrifying, what happened?" asks Mom.

"Oh just. I couldn't move, but I was awake," I explain. "Oh alright well we should probably get going anyway. Visiting hours are almost over and I want to check in with the Hawthorns," says Dad. Visiting hours over? I look at the internal clock on my phone. It's a quarter to four. I slept for nearly three hours, and yet it seemed like I just dozed. What was that thing though? That entity I saw. It's as if it was *watching* Adam, but why? Was it just a nightmare, or some kind of omen?

4: The Funeral

Denise's funeral is the first I've ever been to. It is being held outdoors in the local cemetery, and since we aren't part of a congregation (the only time we even make the trip is for the High Holy Days), Dad is leading the ceremony as lay leader in place of a Rabbi. I'm surprised at the number of family members that flew out here on such short notice, but there are no less than four additional families related to the Hawthorns here for the funeral.

Only a few people of our community were invited to come, including us, the sheriff, the Willows, The Sourwoods, and a few other individuals. Many other families have their own funerals to attend, and others like the Larches simply aren't welcome. I offered to play some songs on my guitar for the funeral, but Mrs. Hawthorn says that some of their family members might look down upon music or anything celebratory at a funeral. We aren't even allowed to bring flowers!

I specifically told Mom that I want flowers and music and junk food at my funeral. I want to go out with a bang, but this funeral just makes me feel worse about Denise. It's only been three days since the accident and it feels like there has been no real preparation other than chairs and the coffin lying before us. I'm sitting in the front row, but the rest of my family (aside from my Dad), sits in the middle section, making room for the Hawthorn's relatives to take their seats up front.

I look at Dad standing before the coffin. He's reciting prayers, but I can barely hear him. I'm lost in my own train of thought. *What do we do now?* I think. *Do we just move on, carry on like normal? Or will things be different now? Empty?*

As I think, I look around at all of the faces looking at my father. I'm surprised to say there aren't that many people looking directly at him. Many are looking at the ground, others at their hands, and even some of them are looking around like me. I look and see Leanne Sourwood, the girl who keeps trying to show me up on track. She has short blonde hair that comes down to her ears, and bright blue eyes. I won't say she's spoiled, she does work hard, but she also likes to use that to one-up people, and even today she's wearing the most casual dress clothes on the market. It's as if she has no time to dress for a funeral, as if she's beyond them. My dress comes down to my knees, and I have tights that cover my legs down to shiny black pumps. Right now she's staring at me angrily as if I've done something to her. We're excused from school until the funeral finishes, and so I haven't had the chance to use Shana's idea to beat her in a race, but she's still glaring at me. Is she jealous of something? I look away, trying not to make this funeral seem awkward.

After Dad finishes reciting the passages, they lay Denise into the grave, and we all line up to pour a shovelful of earth into it. Since I sat in the first row, I am one of the first lined up to take their turn. As I approach, one of the funeral staff hands me a spade, and I scoop up a shovelful of dirt and place it upon Denise's still very visible coffin. The dirt splashes against the coffin, not even making a dent in filling up the grave. I hand the shovel to one of Shana's relatives behind me, and move on. I stand and watch as everyone takes their turn with the spade. Some of their relatives cry, or say a quick farewell as they take their turn. Others remain silent and solemn.

When Leanne is handed the spade, she looks reluctantly at the grave, as if she doesn't want anything to do with the burial, but she quickly recovers from her hesitation and dumps a hefty amount of soil into the grave before handing it back to her mother. Leanne didn't lose anyone related to her in the crash, but I've heard that she lost a baby brother to pertussis sometime before I moved here, but she never talks about it. Either way, it's probably not the first time she's had to deal with something like this. Leanne and her mother are the only Sourwoods that came, and lined up behind them are the Willows. The Willows didn't lose any of their children in the crash. Their youngest is four, and an only child. When everyone in the line has taken their turn, the grave is still nowhere near filled. It's now that Dad ushers some of the mourners to stand around the grave and recite the burial Kaddish. Most of the people around the grave are Denise's family members, in fact I think my Dad- who's leading the ceremony, is the only one not directly related. After the burial Kaddish, he leads all of us- at least those of us that know the words (not including me) into the mourning Kaddish, while the hired funeral staff takes over filling the rest of the grave.

After the burial, Dad hosts a memorial session, and throughout the whole event I can feel Leanne's eyes boring holes into my neck. I catch her looking at me twice, and then avert my gaze, knowing she's still looking at me. If I've done something to set her off, I don't know what it could be. After the memorial, I decide to confront her.

When most of the audience drifts around the site, not wanting to be the first family to leave, I approach Leanne. I tap her on the shoulder and she turns around to face me. It's only when I get this close to her that I realize just how pallid her complexion is. She barely has any more color on her skin than Adam. She looks me up and down, sizing me up, as if she hadn't noticed me all day, and wonders why I have the audacity to purse my lips at her like this. She raises her eyebrows. I hold my hands out and shake my head.

"I don't like passive aggressiveness Leanne. What is it?" I say. She cocks her head to the side as if not sure how to respond to my approach. I can tell she originally intended to play dumb for her initial response, but is intuitive enough to know that I'm ready to skip that.

"I don't like you," she finally says.

"It seems like more than that. You don't stare at someone for hours just because you don't like them. You look like you want to kill me. Like you hate me. Why?" I ask.

Now Leanne purses her lips.

"Look around you," she says. I look around.

"Everyone here has lost something. Everyone except you," she continues.

The Slender Man

"You don't think I'm suffering from this?" I ask.

"Your phony empathy can't compare to real suffering. You're just playing along, not sure how to handle it. You think you're the lucky one," she answers.

"Are you saying that Adam should have died too?" I ask, getting angry.

Her eyes tell me that *is* the truth, but her mouth doesn't want to admit it out loud.

"I'm just saying it's not fair that you all got to cheat your way out of it. This is one of three funerals I'm going to, but this is probably the only one you'll go to. Am I right?" she asks snidely.

"Cheat my way out of it? What do you-"

"That's because you don't care about the dead children. The only reason you're here is because of Shana, out of respect, but you don't feel any loss for her sister."

"How can you say that? They're like family to me."

"But they're not your family. You haven't suffered any real loss. You think Lady Luck is on your side, but it's about time- oh," she stops and puts her hand to her face.

I narrow my eyes and try to figure out what's wrong, and then I see it. I see a little trickle of red running from between her fingers. She's having a sudden nosebleed. I think about offering help, but after her selfish reasoning over how I didn't lose Adam or care about Denise, I really don't think I should. She pushes past me, I guess to get a tissue, but the closest building to the funeral site is the funeral parlor which is a few hundred feet away, so she breaks into a jog. It almost mimics the speed she runs in front of me on track.

Something catches my eye. I look and see Lionel Willow running around the graveyard, seemingly unattended. Lionel is pretty short, even for a four year old, and the puff of curly brown hair on his head is almost as big as his face, but it's not him that catches my eye. I walk over to investigate closer and as I approach I almost see it. It's mid-afternoon, bright daylight so you can see through the lightly spaced tree line, but in one area, in one gap, you can hardly see anything. Instead there is blackness. It's not just a shadow; it's out of place, like someone is standing there. Could it be someone hiding behind a tree? No with the way the sun is positioned, from behind the trees, the shadow would be cast toward us. This one is in one spot. I walk over to it, hoping it's just a trick of the eye.

As I get closer I can see that the shadow is moving, and I recognize the movement. It's got those violent, jagged contortions like the static being from my dream. Only this time it's not as vivid or as clear. If not for the incident in the hospital, I probably would think it's all in my head.

The Slender Man

I walk over to Lionel and he looks up at me. I've only met Lionel a few times, mostly on special occasions, and every time I meet him he gives me a big baby-toothy grin and says

"Hi." This time Lionel stops moving and begins to cry. I squat down and put my hand on his shoulder. He's starting to wail and I heard a pair of footsteps approach. Mrs. Lionel comes swooping in and picks him up.

"What are you doing way out here?" she asks him, but more in a cooing manner than scolding him. She looks at me quizzically.

I shake my head and say "I saw him running around over here and came to get him then he freaked," I explain.

"Oh, but he loves you! Maybe something spooked him. This isn't a very happy environment," she explains with a grin just as toothy as her son's. Her teeth are bright white. In fact, it looks unnatural, but with her being a dentist I guess you can expect that. He begins coughing and a spot of blood appears on her neck.

"Oh I see," she says.

"Someone's allergies are acting up, huh?" she says in that same cooing manner. I give a forced smile and she nods back at me before patting him on the back and walking back over to the others.

At that I remember why I came over here and look back to the tree line. The being is gone, but I can still... feel it. I look around the trees from my position and when I don't see anything, I turn back around. Is it really the same thing I saw in that dream? I wonder. I know my eyes aren't playing tricks on me. Maybe it is some kind of omen? Maybe Death is watching over us hungry for more? I begin to walk back and notice the place is starting to clear out. I don't see any of the Sourwoods and it looks like the Willows are about to take their leave as well. In fact, even the cemetery staff seems to be done with their job. I guess that's my cue to catch up with my family.

On my way I see Shana and decide to go and talk to her. When I approach she looks up at me, but I'm still ten feet away and didn't want to risk saying anything she wouldn't hear and trigger an awkward moment. I hold my arms out as I clear the remaining distance and she accepts my hug with no hesitation. She isn't crying, but I can tell the pain of losing her sister hasn't dulled any from the day it happened.

"I'm sorry for your loss," I say for the tenth time. I feel like since I'm her best friend, I should have more things to say than what everyone else has already said.

"Do you want me to stay over for shivah?" I ask. Sitting shivah is another custom I don't like. It's when the mourning family stays in their house and well, mourns, devoid of anything that would be considered pleasurable. They don't use hot water, shave, listen to music, or even leave the house for a whole week! The only interaction they will even get is from visitors like me and my family. It's another custom I don't want my family to uphold, because all it will do is hurt them further after my death. Some may not feel that way. Some may use the shivah as it's intended, to set aside an official period of time suitable for mourning and to let it all out, but not me. It takes a while for her to muster a response, and she starts by shaking her head.

"Yeah, but some of my relatives will still be in town visiting for the first couple days, so not until Thursday. I need you to let the school know I won't be back for a week," she explains.

Oh right... school. It's Tuesday today and we have that essay to write. We haven't even started it, but I think Ms. Alder will forgive us in light of the circumstances. That is, unless she shares Leanne's point of view on my brother's survival.

"Don't listen to Leanne," she says, as if hearing my thoughts.

"Huh?" I say.

"I overheard what she said. Don't listen to it. There's no reason for her to believe that it's not fair Adam's okay," she says.

"Equal isn't always fair," I say in response.

"Alyssa, it's time for us to get going, we need to give the Hawthorn's some space with their family," Dad calls. I turn and nod at him, then turn back to Shana. "

See you Thursday?" I ask. She gives me a forced smile and nods.

"Bring food," she says. I turn back and head toward my family. As I walk, my mind hops back to Leanne. If that's the way that she really feels, then what about the others? Will all of them resent me?

5: The Sickness

I walk through the entrance of my school. The Cherokee County board of education is *very* creative with its school names. Here we have Murphy Elementary, Murphy Middle, and my school, Murphy High. It's very shoddy though, and many residents of Murphy try to enroll their children into the high school in Andrews; Andrews High. I remember late last year when I walked through these doors in September. I bought into the myth that everyone would size me up and shun me because of my freshman status and that I'd have twenty pairs of eyes boring into my neck. I soon tossed that aside, but now I am expecting those same burning gazes, not because I'm a freshman walking into the high school building for the first time, but because I'm the "Lucky One." I am the only one of around fifteen students that didn't lose a sibling in the crash. There are people in all grades that would happily switch places with me, and like Leanne, they may resent me because that won't happen.

I head straight into my first class, English. I walk into the doors and I am almost relieved to see that Leanne is absent. That little bit of relief drops when I see that Jason Larch is here, and he's giving me that hateful glare I've been anticipating all morning. What I wouldn't give to have Shana walking in with me right now. I try not to look at anyone else as I find my way to my desk, but I can sense more than one pair of eyes on me.

It's five minutes till class starts and it looks like Ms. Alder is in a hurry to prepare something. She looks away from her work just quickly enough to see me about to sit at my desk.

"Welcome back Alyssa," she says.

"Th-thank you," I stammer. I'm a little nervous about Ms. Alder, hoping that she won't bring up the creative history essay that's overdue. I look around at the other students and see that most of them are looking at the books on their desk or whispering amongst each other like normal. So that helps my mood a bit. I just hope that the gossip of the week isn't on me.

The Slender Man

"Alright class, it seems that many of the students still haven't returned, but we can't delay any longer. Please open your books to chapter thirty," she says. I realize that I don't know which book she means, but rather than asking on impulse, and drawing attention to myself. I steal a gaze to my right and see that everyone is opening their literature books. It's a good thing I looked, because if I had to guess I would have opened grammar

Ms. Alder is a stout woman, but not really fat. She looks like a woman that simply doesn't have the will to exercise but still doesn't eat too much, and at her age it's starting to take its toll. She has short sandy brown hair and bangs that cover half of her forehead, which is a little too big. She wears contacts, but with her physique, she'd look better off with actual glasses. She acts as both our history and our English teacher, which is where my whole dual-subject assignment comes from. She leads us through the next chapter, which is on multicultural literature, a topic that generally bores me. Her class isn't very interactive as she reads from the text verbatim, so my mind wanders. I guess that's why my grades are falling.

I look around and see Jason Larch just about as entertained as I am. *Didn't he get arrested?* I think. Why did the sheriff let him off so easily? He's normally not a pushover. I notice that Jason has a little bruise on his nose, but it doesn't look broken.

Something peculiar about that bruise is how visible it is from ten feet away. I realize that his skin has paled a bit, quite like Leanne's. She had a nosebleed, and so did Lionel, who's also paled. Is everyone getting sick? I take my attention from him and notice that very few of the other students appear sick. In fact, even Lindsay Willow isn't sick looking, and she has been around Lionel. Must not be a very contagious thing though, otherwise I'd have it by now, because my immune system is terrible and I get sick at least every quarter.

After Ms. Alder reads the chapter to us, she stands up and offers a fifteen minute break to everyone. Most of the kids jump up as they have a sudden realization that they are about to wet themselves and they're dying of thirst, and pretty soon, it's just Ms. Alder and me. *I should get up and go too,* I think, but as I do she addresses me.

"Hey Alyssa, we missed you this week," she says.

"Yeah, sorry," I say, even though we did have permission to skip school due to the accident.

"It's not too much to hope you've finished your essay?" she asks. I cringe, that's the subject I've been dodging.

"No, Shana and I were gonna work on it, and make stories that work together but-,"

"Don't worry, only three students have turned in their essays on time, but I do need yours by the end of the week, and Shana's too," she says, and that reminds me.

"Oh, um, Shana won't be able to," I say.

"Her family is sitting shivah- in mourning and it's a custom that they don't leave the house for a week," I continue.

"Well if she's at home she can work on it there, and you can bring it for me?" she suggests.

"They're really not supposed to do any work during the shivah," I say.

"Well just run it by her," she says. I nod.

"Can you help me with this?" she asks, opening the classroom closet. I stand up and walk over to her and as I get over there, she's hauling a television set out.

"What do you want me to do?" I ask.

"Find me The Joy Luck Club in there? My eyes aren't the best," she explains. I look and see that it's a pretty old television set, and pretty small. I wonder how she thinks even the front row students will see it well.

I go into the closet and sort through the mess inside. It's full of extra textbooks, pencils, and other items for school, and with no sort of organization. No wonder she's having trouble finding a single DVD in here. I look around a bit and realize that there don't seem to be any DVD cases in sight. Then I realize that The Joy Luck Club is an old movie, and that's an old television. So I'm probably looking for a VHS cassette. After making that realization, I see a line of VHS boxes, but a lot of them are empty. In fact, there are a few cassettes strewn about. Isn't there supposed to be some student body president to fix these kinds of problems? Maybe I should say something about this to my Dad, the vice principal and see if he can get the school's equipment up to date, or at least organized.

I find the movie, or at least think I do. The sticker on the tape is pretty badly faded, but I'm sure I can make out the title with what remains of the tape.

"Here," I say, handing the cassette to Ms. Alder. She takes it and puts it into the VCR she just hooked up underneath the television. I see that some of the students are filing back into the classroom.

"Is there anything else you need?" I ask, brushing myself off, although the closet isn't as dusty as you'd think.

"No that should do it. Take your seat please," she says. After a few button pushes, she starts the movie. She lets it run through the previews, which I think is a tremendous waste of class time alongside a full fifteen minute break. During the previews, Jason returns to the room, and he stares me down for a few seconds before taking his seat. He's got some toilet paper stuffed into one of his nostrils. So he has a nosebleed too. I guess that's why Ms. Alder didn't render a *"What took you so long?"*

The Slender Man

My seat is at an angle from the television, but I can see it pretty well. After the previews though, something triggers a sense of unease with me. At first, I think my arm is just falling asleep, but it starts to feel more like a static tingling, and it courses through me like wind. I instinctively look around for that static shadow, but I don't see it. What I do see is Jason stifling a cough and the girl sitting next to him inching away in disgust, as if she's afraid he'll contaminate her. The static wave- I should say, is gone by now, but I see some of the other students in the class squirming about in a similar manner, as if they felt it too.

I turn my attention to the movie and realize what we've been subjected to, a long, boring drama that we will probably have to write an essay about. My body releases a yawn at the thought and I realize that I feel sleepy- very sleepy. I wasn't feeling tired at all this morning, not with the nervousness of being hated, so a sudden need to fall asleep at my desk comes off as a little strange to me. The movie- or 'feature presentation' begins, but as the drowsiness sets in deeper, the sound starts fading. I fight to keep my eyelids open, and see that the sound is distorting into static bursts.

Ms. Alder gets up and begins toggling the cords, but it only worsens as the video starts going out. I hear a groan. Is someone really disappointed that we don't get to watch this movie? I turn and see

Jason, eyes closed, but twitching. He groans again, and twitches a little more. I think I know what's happening. The fit I had in the hospital when I dozed off and saw that entity for the first time. Jason's having it now. I contemplate waking him up, but figure someone like him probably deserves to be stuck in a nightmare for a few minutes. I wonder if he's dreaming about shadows and static too. Then my mind hops back to the television.

It strikes me as odd that after I and probably some of the other students felt a wave of static pass through us, and then the television- that Ms. Alder is ferociously trying to fix with the all-powerful toggle method, distorts, Jason would be having a nightmare. The static actually seems to come from his direction. At the thought, another wave hits me. The drowsiness I'd only just managed to knock off comes again, and this time, I keep my eyes closed for about two seconds to see if it will help.

When I open my eyes, the fiend is there. It's right in front of Jason, and looming over him. It's slim and shadowy, and looks like it could be a person if not for the way its body contorts and shakes like- like static, giving it an indefinite form. It's all black from what I can see and I only look at it for a second before I react with a loud gasp. I blink, and it's gone, but Jason is awake and looking at me. In fact, everyone is looking at me. Some of them look tired and confused, others look annoyed, but Jason's gaze is different. It's not the hateful one that he and Leanne have been giving me. It's a gaze that says

"So you saw it too?

"Alyssa?" says Ms. Alder. She's been toying with the television, and now the video is back on, except not as good a quality as it originally was. *Did it leave?* I think. Ms. Alder is giving me a quizzical look.

"Oh, yeah. There was spider, it was tiny, but it crawled into my sleeve... and startled me, sorry," I say. Ms. Alder nods.

"Try and keep quiet," she says. Throughout the rest of the class we watch the movie in its horrible half-visible quality. I hope she doesn't expect us to do an essay on this, because even when I do try and pay attention I don't understand anything that's happening. For the most part, I'm too busy thinking about that thing that I- and now possibly Jason, have seen. After class, we have lunch period, and I'm on my way when I get grabbed from behind. It's Jason. He pushes me against a wall.

"You saw him?" he asks.

"H-him?" I stammer. I've never been intimidated by Jason, but he's never gotten in my face and held me against a wall before. He's putting a lot of weight against my shoulder, and it kind of hurts, but I don't think that's his intention. Still, I'm contemplating using my pepper spray on him, but

I'm not sure it's a bad enough situation to risk having my only self-defense item confiscated over.

"Don't play dumb. You saw Kenny too?" he growls.

"No, I didn't see him," I answer truthfully. Was his nightmare about Kenny?

"You looked right at him and then screamed," he presses.

"No, I, it wasn't him," I choke, trying to push his hand off. He doesn't move.

"Hey!" I hear. Jason and I both look and see none other than my dad. He's looking Jason dead in the eye and frowning at him, but it's an angry frown, that's meant to be intimidating, but looks more like a moping face. "Get your hands off my daughter," says Dad.

Jason jerks away from me, and storms off, but not before giving me one more glare and saying, "He wants my help, and I'm gonna do it," he says.

"What?" I ask, but he's got his back turned to me now.

"Are you alright," asks Dad.

"Yeah, yeah, he's just-"

"No excuses, if he touches you again knock his lights out, and I'll have him arrested," he interrupts. I wonder how exactly Dad expects me to *knock the lights* out of someone like Jason, but I just give him a nod.

"Roger," I say.

The Slender Man

"I came to get you," he continues.

"Come on, we're going to get Adam, they're letting him go," he says. My eyes light up. Adam's finally coming back! They said they'd only need him for a couple more days, but it's the fifth day. I don't hesitate, I don't argue, I don't even grab my backpack, and my dad and I are in the car on the way to the hospital in less than five minutes.

At the beginning of the drive to Andrews, I feel joyous, and am highly anticipating getting to hug my little brother again when he's awake, but later in the ride, I have time to think. I think about that static entity I've seen thrice now. I've seen it too many times for it to be some kind of hallucination, as I'm not on any medication to induce them, and although the recent events have downed me severely, I'm not depressed enough to conjure them.

The only possible solutions I am able to think up, are that either A: it's some kind of ghost, or entity like the Boogeyman; or B: it's got something to do with the disease that's making everyone pale and giving them nosebleeds, which doesn't add up as much even though it would be the more scientifically acceptable solution. Then I am struck with worry. If it is an omen, and I saw it first at the hospital, does that mean something is going to happen to Adam?

We pull up to the community hospital, and my door is open before the car comes to a full stop.

"Whoa, careful!" shouts Dad, but I am already walking a brisk pace to the hospital. I don't want to make a scene, because it's only a hunch, but the tension is building up inside.

When I get indoors, I don't stop at reception, I don't check the map on the wall. My feet guide me exactly where I need to go from memory. I make a numerous rights and lefts with the white walls decorated with portraits of nameless child models mark my path. When I get to one of a two little kids shooting each other with water pistols I recall the almost concealed door to the stairway. I open the gray door and go up two flights, after a few more turns here and there I'm in the hallway we awaited the fate of our loved ones in. I don't enter the intensive care ward though. I continue until I get to the end of the hall, and make another left.

There are two double doors on my right. They lead to the recovery ward. I am about to enter when I hear my dad's voice in conversation with someone, but they aren't behind me. *Ding!* I look to the left and see an elevator door open, and my Dad steps through accompanied Dr. Spruce, now with a happier look on her face. I am ready to face-palm myself. *The elevator!*

"…here she is. I'm telling you she just took right off!" says Dad to Dr. Spruce.

"Eager to see her little brother?" she smiles. I nod back and she leads us through the recovery ward. I don't take off this time, lest they have some teleportation device that will get us there faster, but they don't. We enter Adam's room and I am surprised to see him already out of bed in a wheelchair being pushed by the nurse that almost wordlessly relayed the fate of Kenny to the Larches. I look at Adam with a smile, but it drops quickly as I see that not only is he not smiling back, but no color has returned to his face, and he puts a bloody tissue up to his nose stifling a nosebleed.

6: The Sadness

Vegetable alfredo and falafel sticks with hummus. I smell the aroma of the food resting in my arms, and can almost taste it. We cooked this for the Hawthorn's and are bringing it to them. It's not traditional for people to use appliances while sitting shivah, so family and friends often bring meals during visits. The aroma is mouthwatering, and I can't wait to eat it. I am riding in the car driven by my parents. Bubbe is staying at home to watch Adam (she isn't too close to the Hawthorns), but the rest of us are paying a visit, and we will be every day until Wednesday, when the Hawthorns can return to their business.

The Hawthorns don't live far away, but not far away means driving through the main part of town.

The Slender Man

On the way I look around and note how remarkably grand looking the town is for such a small population. A lot of the buildings are constructed with beige bricks and have their business logos painted, and for some places engraved on the buildings. It all seems older and more crudely built, but when you compare them to the more modern buildings, with bright electric signs in other cities, this place just looks beautiful, more serene. Even the supermarket we are driving by looks like it fits right in.

The drive takes around ten minutes, and when we get there, I am first out the door. We get to the front door and I nudge the doorbell with my elbow. Mrs. Hawthorn opens the door and welcomes us inside with a faint smile. She doesn't look so well. Her normally groomed short hair looks messy, worse than bed hair, and she's without makeup. As much as I missed the Hawthorns, my eagerness to see them turns into worry as I see how dark their house has become, even with the lights on. We enter the house and I look around. I am so used to seeing the wall mirror in their living room, but now it is covered. Their television that's usually on all day is off. Even their coffee table, normally strewn with books or newspapers or whatever they were reading at the time is empty. I dread the day I have to practice shivah.

The others gather about in their living room. Shana walks in and gives me a smile that matches her mother's. She also looks very messy, but it looks like she at least ran her fingers through her hair to keep most of the strands straight. I hand the food to Mrs. Hawthorn who thanks us and then takes it into the kitchen. I walk up and hug Shana. "Missed you," I say.

"Missed you too. It's probably not a good thing to say, but I've wanted your company even more than my relatives'. It's been unbearable," she says. It's a few extra seconds before she lets go. It's only now that I get a good look at her. Her skin color has paled, and although I don't see any signs of a nosebleed, I can tell she is sick. I want to comment on it, ask if she needs us to bring some medicine (although her family probably already has some), but she proceeds to thank my family for coming. We all move into the kitchen as Mrs. Hawthorn and Mom dish out the food to everyone. Shana's eyes actually light up as she sees the falafel sticks. Mom's falafel sticks are one of her all-time favorites.

As we eat, Dad gets the conversation going. It's customary to speak about the deceased during the shivah.

"So," he starts.

The Slender Man

"Denise was always the charmer, wasn't she?" he says. I wince, that's probably not the best way to start the conversation.

Mr. Hawthorn is the first to respond.

"Yep, she was a little gremlin in her younger years. I think we spoiled her a bit," he admits. Good, no tears are coming, at least not yet.

"I remember when we first met. Denise asked me for a quarter so she could play the crane game," says Dad.

Mrs. Hawthorn laughs, but I can tell it's forced "She only played that game once, and hated it because she lost."

"Then we come to find out," Dad continues. "She asked Sarah for a quarter too when I was away," he says.

"She ended up swindling a quarter out of every one of you," says Mr. Hawthorn.

"She even tried Adam," I add in.

"She was clever for a three year old, just imagine if," Mom starts. I can tell she was going to say something along the lines of *"Just imagine what ruse she'd pull three years from now."* It's a little too late, and I can see that I'm not the only one that looked down in my plate in response. Luckily no one bursts out crying at the thought. I think it's mutually understood that Denise is dead though and with the last couple of days when their family visited, they probably have had a lot of practice, both crying it out and trying not to cry.

I look at Shana, trying to make eye contact, and it looks like she's the one taking it the worst. I see that same gloomy gaze she had on her face when we first found out about the accident. I'd hoped she feel a little better about it by now. I know it's normal and perfectly rational for a person to feel like it's the end of the world when one of their family members dies, especially a child, but I hate seeing Shana like this. I've only known her four years, but this girl is like- no she *is* my sister, and her mood rubs off on me like grease. I wish I was sitting next to her, I'd reach over and pat her on the back or something, but she is across from me. I reach over and lightly kick her to get her attention, and when she looks at me, I give her one of those smiles that shows her exactly what's on my mind, empathy, and my desire for her to feel better.

She tries to return the smile, but her mouth only wobbles in response and she looks back at her plate. I see she's only managed to eat half of one of her falafel sticks, and hasn't touched her alfredo. I bite my tongue and look at my half-emptied plate. I wish there's something I could say, or sing, or- I wish I'd brought my guitar, no I wish I was *allowed* to bring it. We could do something like play Complicated, and although it would make her feel worse for a second, I think it would help her cry the rest of it out.

The rest of the meal is full of my parents starting conversations about Denise that end short, at least none of them end on a sour note like the first. Mom and I wash the dishes for the Hawthorns, and my Dad stays with them to keep the mood from becoming awkward. If I was mourning, I sure wouldn't want to wait for my best friend to clean up before speaking to her again. I'm sad to say that it isn't just the food on Shana's plate that had to be dumped down the garbage disposal. I think the Hawthorn's have become good at hiding just how hurt they still are by the tragedy.

I hear coughing, and recognize Shana's voice behind it. She is sick too, but her parents aren't.

"My, oh my," comments Mom, drying her hands off on a towel now that we've finished the rest of the dishes.

"I swear everyone's getting sick. Do you think the flu is going around?" she asks.

"I've never had a nosebleed from the flu," I answer, and realize how rude I just sounded.

"I think it's something else. The people I've seen don't appear nauseas, just..,"

"Weak and sad," Mom finishes for me.

"Yeah," I say, her words ringing a note in my mind. Mom and I head back into the living room, and we see Dad chatting with Mr. and Mrs. Hawthorn, but I don't see Shana.

"She went upstairs," says Mrs. Hawthorn, who saw me looking. I nod and begin to head upstairs.

The Hawthorn's house is very different from ours. They have wooden stairs with no carpeting on them unlike our house. At the top of the stairs, the lights are off, and the place is just as dark as it feels. Shana's room is down the hall on the left, and the only light upstairs is coming from it. I walk over to the door, which is slightly ajar, and push it open.

Shana is sitting on her bed, crying. She has a tissue in her hand, and she's using it to wipe the tears from her face, but I can see spots of blood on it. I walk over and sit on the bed with her. We make eye contact, and although I can't find the right words to say, I get my message across. "Shut the door," she says. I get up and do so. I see Shana's guitar case resting in the corner behind the door. There's a little bit of dust on it, so I know she hasn't touched it. I don't think I could have followed that rule of Shivah though. If Adam died, the first object to help comfort me would be my guitar.

"I wish we could play," I admit. Shana is crying harder, she's sobbing now. "Shana, what's-what can I do to help?" I ask, sitting back down and rubbing her shoulder.

"I think I'm going crazy," she says.

The Slender Man

"No, it's normal to feel this way." I say, but even I'm not sure if that's true. She looks at me and shakes her head. "It's not normal to see things," she says.

"See... It's not normal to see?"

"No, I'm seeing... her," she says. I turn my head when she says that.

"Denise?" I ask, even though that's the obvious answer.

I catch her nod out of my peripheral vision. "I can't go an hour without her appearing. I can't sleep without her coming for me," she says.

"Have you told your parents?" I ask.

She shakes her head. "I can't... I've tried crying it out, and I've tried ignoring her, but she won't go away," she explains.

"Maybe you should try talking about-" but I stop, realizing what I am saying. I really am no good at words.

"It's not like I'm just seeing her around though. She's... haunting me," she says.

"Haunting?" I ask. She nods, wiping another tear from her cheek.

"Yeah, like I've done her some wrong," she says. I look down at the bed, thinking, but she grabs my shoulder and looks me directly in the eye. "She wants something," she says.

"Do you know what it is she wants?" I ask.

"At first, even before the funeral... she wanted my help. Now I think she's angry." The word 'help' rings a bell. Jason said that Kenny needed his help, and that he was going to help him, but how?

"She won't let me sleep, she won't let me eat. She's in my dreams, she wants me to leave," she continues.

"Leave? She wants you to go somewhere to help her?" I ask.

"She wants me to go into the forest," she answers.

"What's in the forest?" I ask. She shrugs.

"I don't know. I don't think she's ever been there. I think I'm just... losing it."

I shake my head instinctively. I never recalled anything unusual or significant in the woods. There's nothing like a graveyard or historical event that anyone would take an interest to there. Then again, I've never been deep into the woods. I mostly have only been there for a run, and even the trail I found was only by chance. I missed the bus from school so I took the trail home instead of calling my parents. When I found that the trail turned off course, I just cut through the woods, and came out a quarter mile from my neighborhood. If there is something in there, anything of importance, I've never seen or heard anything about it. I look up and realize that Shana is still waiting for a verbal answer.

The Slender Man

"I think it's just the emotional stress of the situation. I'd be seeing things too," I say.

"I've been seeing things," I correct, thinking of the entity I've been seeing, the one that Jason thought was Kenny.

She shakes her head though.

"I can feel her. When she touches me it... it hurts," she says. Then a thought hits me.

"Does Denise look... normal? When you see her?" I ask.

She shakes her head again.

"She's dark now. It's like she's shrouded in death," she answers.

"When she touches you... is it like being shocked?" I ask.

Her eyes widen.

"You've seen her too!?" she asks loudly, amazement in her eyes.

I shake my head quickly, realizing her excitement may not be such a good thing.

"No, I've just. I've seen something else, but it's never... talked to me, or anything, it's like it's talking to someone else," I answer, but suddenly wish I hadn't said that either.

"Who's it been talking to?" Shana asks. I want to say Jason. After all it's my instinct to tell Shana the truth.

"I can't hear it, but when I saw it, it's like it was talking to… Leanne."

"Well her baby brother got sick and died. Maybe," she thinks aloud, but stops. She must not be sure what conclusion she should come to.

"Shana, let's just not worry about it, I'm sure that with time. With time Denise will go away. How are you feeling? Do you need medicine for your sickness?" I ask, trying to veer off topic.

She shakes her head.

"We got some already. I've been taking antihistamine," she answers.

"It's not working though," she admits.

"Then tomorrow I'll try and bring some Dayquil or something," I say.

"Bring Nyquil," she says. Oh right, she can't sleep. I can see Shana's mind is still on what to do about her sister. I know in my mind that Shana seeing her sister, Jason seeing his brother, and me seeing… what I've been seeing, is no coincidence. There's something going on.

"Oh yeah. Ms. Alder wants you to finish your essay. I told her you couldn't but she wanted me to ask anyway. I have to get mine done tonight," I say, staying off the Denise topic.

She shakes her head and reaches under the bed. "Our relatives all visited at once, each afternoon. I had to do something to pass the time when I ignored Denise," she says. She pulls out a small pile of papers from underneath the bed.

The Slender Man

"You did your essay?" I whispered in surprise. In shivah you're not supposed to work *or* do schoolwork.

"I did *our* essays. Just don't tell my parents," she says, handing me a few of the papers.

"You'll want to copy it down yourself though, so it's in your handwriting, and I put some spelling errors in there for you too." I smile at her as I stuff the essay in my shirt. This is at least one good sign that Shana is still Shana.

"You want me to sneak you your homework too?" I chuckle.

She moves her head back and forth as if pondering.

"Just come? Keep me company?" she says. I nod.

"Every day," I say. She smiles.

"I haven't seen Denise once since you guys came.

"We tend to ward evil spirits away," I joke. The door opens, and I turn to see Mom entering.

"We need to get going," she says rather glumly. Perhaps they ran out of good things to say about Denise and can't handle the awkward silence any more. Before I can respond, Shana hugs me tight.

"Come here straight from school." I am about to ask if she still wants food but then I realized just how little she ate of her favorite dishes today and figure I won't say anything.

"Promise. I'll walk if I have to," I say. Mom escorts me downstairs and we see Dad putting his jacket on, saying his goodbyes to the Hawthorns. Mom and I take our turn and then head out. Dad has already started the car. The drive home is silent, aside from the radio talk show. It's a local radio channel and three guesses on what's still the main subject for the local news? Right.

As I gaze out the window my mind is stuck on Denise, or at least the Denise-apparition. I've got to figure out what's really going on. Maybe the hallucinations really have something to do with the sickness, or maybe ghosts are just real? I've always taken an agnostic approach to ghosts and things like that, but if these visions aren't ghosts, then what are they?

As we get close to home the radio starts to fade out. Static! I look right and left, looking for... it. Dad is closing in on our driveway when he slams on the brakes. Does he see it?

"Adam!" he roars. He and Mom both jump out of the car. I follow suit. We get out and I walk up to them. There is Adam, cast and all, walking in the middle of the road. It's like he didn't even see us! As I approach, my parents are saying things like

"What's wrong with you?" "Where's your Bubbe?" or

The Slender Man

"You're going to tear open your stitches," but I'm not focused on them. I'm still looking for it, but I can't find it, or sense it, anywhere.

"I'm going to check on Hannah," says Dad. "Alyssa, take your brother inside," he orders as he busts in through our already open front door. Mom goes back to take care of the car. I walk over and take Adam's good hand, but it's limp, as if he's not holding back. He's not even looking at me, or us. He's looking down the road... at the forest. Suddenly his hand shocks me. Not a normal contact shock, but that static wave comes through me. He snaps out of it before giving me a confused and terrified look, but he doesn't say anything. He starts to walk along with me, and we go inside the house.

I can hear Dad yelling at Bubbe.

"What were you doing letting him run around in the road? He shouldn't have been out of bed at all!"

"Well I tried to feed the child but he was too sleepy so I laid him down and went up to bed myself!" she shouts back. I decide to let them argue as I escort Adam upstairs and back into bed. It's not her fault. It's something to do with that static shadow, these ghosts, and the illness that's going around. After I tuck him in I feel something slide out of my shirt and I check to see the front page of the essay Shana wrote in my name has fallen.

"Oh right, gotta copy this," I say reluctantly. I chuckle to myself. If I'm too lazy to copy it, then I'd have had no chance to write it myself. Where would I be without Shana? My little moment of humor leaves me as I see the despairing topic she wrote about; The Salem Witch Trials.

7: The Tree

I don't like how melancholy Shana's essays are. The first time we were discussing the project the mood was cheerful, but when I look at these essays I feel saddened. It feels like Shana really does have ghosts haunting her, almost dictating what she writes. Our roles in the Salem Witch Trials are very different. She's one of the women accused of witchcraft, and gets executed for it, but I am a woman who only sympathizes with the witches. I feel like that plays into what happened when she lost Denise, and I kept Adam. She's not jealous, but she's been hit harder than I have.

The story tells about how she's accused and I work hard to protest and defend her, but in the end I'm hanged as well. *Is she trying to tell me something with this?* Is that why she wrote the essays so diligently? Is this her way of telling me not to help her? It's ironic, I can figure out that something supernatural is going on around here quickly, but I can't read in between the lines my best friend has written.

I almost don't want to turn these essays in, but if I care about our grades, then I really have no choice. Beggars can't be choosers, as my Bubbe likes to remind me when I'm being picky. I'm walking from the bus to the school with Shana's essay, and my copied version, when I see something. There is a cop questioning one of the students at the school. I get closer and recognize the officer as Deputy Yew, the policeman who drove Shana and me to the hospital.

When I enter his field of vision he looks up at me and waves me over. I walk up to him and catch the last phrase of his conversation.

"...then let me know if you hear anything. Thanks... Alyssa," he says.

"Good morning," I greet. He didn't cut himself when he shaved this morning.

"I'm afraid I have some more bad news," he said. *Bad news? About who*? It can't be Adam or anyone in my family because I saw them not thirty minutes ago. Wait a minute. Shana!

"Is she alright?" I ask immediately.

"She? Who? This is about Mr. Douglas, and some missing students," he says.

"Oh, go on," I say, relieved.

"We've received reports of some missing children, teenagers mostly. We can't launch a formal investigation, but all of the missing teens are related to some of the deceased," he explains. I nod.

"Alright, now one of those missing teens is Jason Larch," he says.

Jason is missing, that doesn't sound like bad news to me.

"Jason had a court date this morning that he missed, even his parents showed up. They assumed he was with a friend," he continues. *Well that's what you get when you don't raise your kids right.*

"It just so happens, that Mario Douglas was reported missing from the hospital around three in the morning last night. The hospital staff say Mario was about to be released as he had some relatives ready to take care of him, but he disappeared," he says.

"So you think Jason and the others had something to do with this?" I ask.

"Yes, and we're hoping maybe you've seen any of these kids? Jason is the only one in your grade, but do you recognize the other two?" he asks. He shows me pictures of Jason and two girls that look a little older than me. There is a fourth picture in his hand, but it's of a chubby boy that looks like he might be in the fourth or fifth grade. Jason looks like the only one that would be interested in murdering Mr. Mario, but I guess you can't judge people by their pictures.

"I'm sorry, Jason is the only one I recognize, and I haven't seen him since yesterday when…" I stop. *Jason said he was going to help Kenny!* "He told me he was seeing his brother," I say.

"You mean like…"

"Like he saw his brother in class, and he said that his brother needed his help. He told me that he was going to help him," I explain.

"Wait, so are you two close? No one I've spoken to has said anything about this," he says.

"No, he- he thought I saw Kenny too because I jumped up in fright from a- a spider. He must have 'seen' Kenny at the same time. He was very aggressive about it. You can ask my Dad."

He raises his hand to stop me. "I believe you. He's not the only one that's reported seeing things and that story about adds up," he says.

"It does?" I ask.

"A few people said they last saw him talking to you, and everyone that's seen him says they last saw him at school yesterday. If he left school planning on helping Kenny, then he might have gathered some followers and planned to sneak into the hospital. It all adds up, we just don't have proof that he's responsible. If you see him, or any of these kids," he says, waving the photos. "...let me know."

"Right, will-do," I say. I hear the bell ring.

"Better run along," says Deputy Yew, but it looks like he's saying it more to himself than to me. I thank him, although I'm not sure what exactly I was thanking him for-information? I shrug it off and head into the school. I get to my classroom as quickly as I can. Before Ms. Alder can greet me with *"Glad you could join us,"* I say, "Sorry was giving information to the deputy."

Ms. Alder looks up at me, and I hand the essays.

"Oh," she says, a little surprised that I- well, Shana, followed through.

"Well, glad you could join us, please take your seat." I wince at those words. I don't know why, but I have this pet peeve where if someone has a certain catchphrase or something they always say, I hate being the one to trigger it. School goes by far too slowly. There's no Dad to bust me out before lunch period. Heck he's probably catching up on the work he missed out on yesterday, whatever vice principals do.

The whole school day I have my mind on what Jason could be doing to Mario right now, and why those other students would help him, if they were helping him. Are they torturing him, or disposing of his body? Those kinds of questions run through my mind incessantly. When the final bell rings, another bell dings in my head. *Time for Shana!* I realize I haven't told my parents that I plan to go see Shana early today, so I go over to the vice principal's office. The door's open so I walk in, on Ms. Alder talking to my Dad, with our essays in hand.

"Oh, Alyssa," greets Dad, and his tone isn't happy sounding.

"What's going on?" I ask.

Ms. Alder gives me a small apologetic smile. "I've just been going over your essays with your father," she explains.

"What's wrong with them?" I ask, although I already know what she's going to say. "Well they…" but she stops and gives my Dad a look. Wow, she can come behind my back and talk about these essays but she won't say it to my face?

"I haven't, read the essays completely Alyssa, but Ms. Alder believes the theme of these essays written by both of you are, well it doesn't seem like two people wrote them," he explains.

So wait, they weren't worried about the style, they just aren't fooled by Shana's trick?

"Well we worked together on them. Like I said yesterday, we were going to use the same event to-"

"Yesterday Alyssa, you hadn't even started your essay, so that means you both would have to have put all of this work into it in one night," she says.

The Slender Man

"In one visit that lasted barely more than an hour, and most of that hour was spent on dinner," corrects my Dad.

"So? What business of yours is it to go over and…" I try, but Ms. Alder interrupts.

"What's the name of the man you were reluctantly arrested by in this essay?" she asks. I hesitate, because I don't know the answer to the question off the top of my head. Wasn't it Turnpin? No wait.

"Turpin?" I ask, although I probably should have declared it.

"That's the name of the judge Alyssa," she says.

"Did Shana write these essays?" asks Dad. He's glaring at me, clearly not ready for any more lies. I just give him a look that says yes, but without fully admitting it. He sighs angrily and rubs his forehead, although you can tell he already knew the truth before I came in.

"This worries me though, the implications here," she continues to my father.

"What implications? They're just essays," I protest. So not only are they not fooled, they are worried about Shana now.

"Alyssa, if you actually bothered to read a single one of the seven pages of this essay," Dad says snidely, "…then you would be worried about your friend too." He doesn't know this, but I am worried about Shana.

"We need to bring this up with her parents. Maybe get her to a psychiatrist," suggests Ms. Alder.

"She doesn't need a shrink, she's just... venting!" I yell.

"Alyssa!" shouts Dad. "Go home," he says.

I am about to turn around before I realize that I had a reason for coming in here.

"Dad, I need to see Shana. I told- I promised I'd head straight for her house right after school," I say.

"Well that's not going to happen young la- little girl," he says, correcting himself with the term *little girl* in order to condescend toward me, and it's working.

"You're lucky if we even take you with us tonight after your Mom finds out about your irresponsibility. Now get out of my face," he continues.

I shrug, with a few tears about to fall. There are a lot of things I want to say, but when my Dad gets like this, he won't hear any of it.

"Probably already missed the bus," I choke.

"Oh, well I can give her a ride," suggests Ms. Alder, but I cut her a hateful glare. The last thing I want to do is accept a ride from the woman who just sold me out.

The Slender Man

"Fine then, walk. Call me- from home, in one hour. When you get home put your cell phone on my desk," says Dad. I storm out of the office, and slam it behind me. *Some help he is.* I walk down the almost empty hallway, barely able to contain my anger as I exit the school. I head to the forest line, but then stop. My hair is down, and I don't have anything to contain it with, plus I'm wearing a skirt and some Chucks, and have no water. I'm in no position to run, or even jog comfortably, and he expects me to be home in an hour. I sigh and move on. Let's hope I can walk through a few miles of woods and get home inside an hour.

As I enter the woods through the dirt trail, I hear the crunching of leaves underneath my feet. It takes me a while to notice, but then I finally stop and look. The trail is almost completely covered in leaves. Most of them still have a little green in them. It's late spring though, and the trees are supposed to be springing- or sprung with leaves right now. I look up at the trees above me and am surprised at just how bare they seem. They usually don't shed this vigorously until autumn, and even then the leaves are generally dead and brown before they fall.

"What's going on?" I say to myself. I continue on down the trail, stomping on the leaves with my eyes pinned on the ground. It's taking me much longer than I remember to follow the trail to the clearing. It must have been years since I actually took the trail route home, so maybe my memory is just foggy.

After way more of my allotted hour than should be is spent, I finally reach that sharp turn, and step off the trail onto my route. I march forward, into the clearing and slip. The extra fallen leaves have hidden those sudden slopes or roots I'm used to seeing out of the corner of my eye and avoiding them. I don't get up instantly. Instead, I pummel the ground with my fists in anger. I want to go see Shana like I promised, but she lives like ten miles from the school, and if I don't call Dad from the home phone, he'll probably head down to the Hawthorns himself. What does he know? If there is really a reason to be worried about Shana (and to be honest, with her visions, there is), then having me there will help her.

I realize I'm only wasting time- although to be honest I am not really worried about making it home within an hour. I jump up to my feet and lean forward against a tree. My vision goes fuzzy and I feel a wave of dizziness hit my head. I must have gotten up too quickly. When my vision returns, I still feel fuzzy and shake out my limbs.

As I do, I notice something. The tree I was just leaning against looms above me. It's not as tall as the other trees, only around fifteen feet tall, but it's very... slender. It's so slim I can probably wrap my hands together around it. It's dark, almost black, and its bark is very rough to the touch. I don't recognize it at all. I look around to make sure that I'm in the right clearing, and aside from the excessive amounts of fallen leaves, and this tree, everything looks familiar. I take a step back to examine the tree.

"What kind of tree is this?" I ask myself aloud. It only has six branches. Two of them hang down perpendicular to each other and almost reach the ground. They are both angled at the same point, as if they're jointed. The other four branches have the same joint shaped, but are angled up and all point away from the tree. At the top of the tree, or head of the tree, is huge, gnarly, bevel. It sticks out like a large tumor.

"There's no way I wouldn't have seen this tree before," I say aloud, and it's true. If I saw a tree this weird-looking before I would have noticed it, just like I do now. It's very creepy.

I realize I've wasted more time and begin to resume my walk. I find my way down the slope, consciously recalling the locations that any roots may be hidden. I'm at the bottom of the hill when I sense something, and turn around. I only look for a second, but there stands the monster at the top of the hill. In that second, so much terror fills my gut, I forget who I am. I just run. I'm not worried about the hair in my face. I'm not worried about the ripping sound my skirt is making, and I'm not worried about the slippery thuds of my Chuck Taylor's landing against the leafy ground. I twist and turn and angle around trees, tripping on roots, but my stride is so wide that I simply land with my next foot before I fall. I feel as if I have to make myself breathe, because if I don't consciously demand it, I'll forget.

I want to look back, to see if it's chasing me, or maybe to see if it's just a trick of the mind, but I'm too afraid to, and with the loud sound of leaves crumbling, branches snapping, and the wind rushing past my face, I'm lucky to hear myself breathe. I run for who knows how long until I see the light at the end of the tunnel. The end of the forest! I have a leaden weight of terror in my stomach as I draw near though. *What if it's just toying with me?* What if it's waiting to pounce and drag me back into the woods, just as I'm about to emerge? I sprint faster, if that's even possible, and close my eyes as I clear the woods. If it does grab me, I don't want to see that horizon dragged away from me. I hear something. It sounds like something screeching. *Oh no! It's coming.*

I hear a loud honk, and open my eyes just in time to see myself run right into a car. It had already stopped moving before I hit it, but my stomach tells me I still ran into it too hard.

The Slender Man

"Alyssa? What is the matter with you?" I hear. I open my eyes. Karen Willow is standing before me, frightened as can be.

"You look like you've seen a ghost. Are you okay?" she asks. The throbbing pain in my stomach subsides a bit before I'm able to speak.

"I thought something was chasing me. I'm not sure what it was," I finally answer.

She looks back at the tree line, eyes wide. "Well I don't see anything, you must have lost it," she says. I chuckle a bit as I think about what I saw. "It might have been a snake. I honestly didn't look at it hard enough to tell," I say without thinking. Did I really see the fiend at the top of the hill with that tree?

No. I laugh again. I saw the tree, that's what spooked me. I let out a small breath.

"Well if it was a snake, it probably took off just as fast as you did-in the other direction," she says.

"Yeah, sorry. Did I hurt your car?" I ask. I look and can't see any apparent damage.

She brushes the hood as if to knock dust off before shaking her head.

"No it looks fine. Say, I just came from your house. I invited your brother to Lionel's birthday party next week. You're welcome to come too. I think Lionel feels bad about how he cried in front of you at the funeral.

"Oh um, sure I'll try and make it." *If I'm not grounded,* I leave out.

"Oh great, he'll love to see you! Anyway I have to head out, try not to run into any more cars," she says before turning to get back inside.

"Alright I'll try," I say with a small smile.

Damn tree.

8: The Disappearance

The ride to Shana's house isn't as happy as I hoped it would be. Dad is barely letting me come today. I don't think he's as mad about the fact that I cheated on the essay as he is about how it makes him look. How would me not bringing one in look? How about that huh? I'm not going to forgive Ms. Alder any time soon. Maybe what I did is wrong, but it's not her business to go out of her way to prove it. It's just a grade.

I'm grounded over the weekend, which normally would be okay with me, seeing as I don't leave the house much anyway, but that means I won't get to see Shana then. The only reason I'm even allowed to go today is because my Mom thinks it's a good idea to be forgiving on the Sabbath.

Adam and Bubbe would have come, but Adam is still sick, and we think it's best she watch over him while we're out. This time Adam sleeps in her room so he won't go on any random trips during the night. When we get to the Hawthorn's, the house is as glum as I feel. Dad greets them with a bright smile and a "Shabbat Shalom," but something is keeping the Hawthorn's from rejoicing- besides Denise's death.

We get inside and see Shana sitting upon a couch, not even looking up at us. Did she get in trouble about the essays too? No Dad said none of us should mention it to them because it would cause unnecessary trouble, and if the teacher or principal called they wouldn't answer the phone, so they wouldn't know from the school either. I walk over to Shana and attempt to hug her, but it takes her a while to figure out what I was doing, and then she only feebly reaches up and hugs back.

"I'm sorry, I tried to come earlier but," I start, but she isn't making eye contact. It's as if she's hardly aware that I'm here. "Is she on any medication?" I ask Mr. Hawthorn. He sighs.

"None that would do this. It's Denise, she keeps mumbling her name. I think maybe she blames herself and it's setting in. We are taking her to see a doctor after the shivah," he explains.

The Slender Man

"Well why not now? She's, it's like she's catatonic," I protest.

"Now Alyssa, this is none of your business. You let them handle Shana and we'll handle you," says Dad. I grind my teeth together. Shana needs help now, and she might not be this way if I'd arrived this afternoon.

"We should get dinner set," says Mom. She and Mrs. Hawthorn head down into the kitchen. Mr. Hawthorn goes back after them. Dad starts to go in.

"Come on," he demands.

"We shouldn't leave her alone," I say, taking her hand and trying to draw a response from her.

"Now, Alyssa," he demands again. Every time he snaps at me my mind flashes to Ms. Alder. I want to slap her, probably just as Dad wants to slap me. I get up and pull on Shana's hand. Slowly, she begins to rise up. She gets on her feet and slowly turns her head in my direction, but she's looking through me. Her demeanor oddly reminds me of Adam's behavior when we caught him wandering through the road last night. With me pulling her hand, she follows. Dad at least doesn't stop me from guiding Shana. He may be irritated with me for the essays, but even he can't deny that something is wrong with Shana, and something that clearly can't wait until Wednesday. I seriously hope they say something during dinner.

We gather around the table and Mom guides everyone through the Motzi. During shivah the mourners still observe the Sabbath, which helps to lighten up the mood a little, but the absence of Shana's... lucidity, ruins the mood, at least for me. Shana doesn't eat at all, not even any of the challah. She does push her food around a bit though.

Today, our parents stay off the topic of Denise, so conversation is easy to carry. The Hawthorn parents keep trying to draw me in, but it seems Dad doesn't want me doing too much talking. When the Hawthorn's ask

"How was school today Alyssa?" he answers for them

"She failed her essay, a big one." It's true that I failed the essay, seeing as I will end up getting a zero, but he's leaving out exactly how I failed the essay.

After dinner, Mrs. Hawthorn says

"Why don't you and Shana go hang out upstairs, we'll take care of cleaning up." I can't tell if she's hoping my presence will help restore Shana's mood, or if she caught onto how awkward Dad is making the conversation. I have to guide Shana upstairs. It's as if my hand tugging on her is the only thing guiding her through her thoughts. When we get up to her room however, she let's go of my hand and walks over to her bed. She sits down on it and pulls her knees in, wrapping her arms around them.

"Is it Denise?" I ask, hoping to draw some kind of conversation out of her.

"Denise, it's not Denise. It's not her," she answers, rocking herself.

"You said you were seeing her."

She looks at me, this time directly in the eye. It looks like she wants to cry, but there are no tears.

"It's not her," she repeats. "Who is it then?" I ask. With that question she stops moving as if to think. She furrows her brow as if she thinks she should know the answer, but it's not coming to her.

I note how dark the circles underneath her eyes are. "Have you been able to get any sleep?" I ask.

"I don't want to sleep," she says, her body rigid with terror.

"Why not? Is that when you see her?" I ask.

"He wants me to sleep," she says.

"Who is he? Who are you seeing?" She bites her lip in response and shakes her head. "Is it the static? It won't let you sleep?" I ask.

She looks back at up at me. She opens her mouth to speak, but then stops. She does this a couple times before finally getting out what she wants to say.

"Don't leave me again." As much as I want to tell her that I won't, my thoughts run to my Dad, and how if I were to dig my nails into the floor, he'd be willing to drag me out. I could kick and scream and he won't be willing to let me stay here. *If I hadn't turned in those essays.* I sit beside her on the bed and put my arm around her.

"I need you to be strong," I say. I feel her shudder. She may not be herself, but she definitely understands what I'm trying to say to her.

"The essays didn't work," I say. I figure if I get her off topic, I can pull her back to herself.

"The essays didn't work," she repeats.

"The essays," she continues. I'm not doing a very good job.

"Why did you choose that story?" I ask.

"The story," she says. I think she's getting worse.

"Shana, listen to me. Why did you write that story?" She doesn't answer. I feel a wave of static pass through me. I know what this is.

"Shana?" I ask. I look at her, and see her eyelids have closed. "Shana!?" I say, trying to wake her up, before she- or even I see it.

She jumps awake and looks at me. She pauses for a moment and then begins panting and trembling. Finally she says.

"Don't leave," again. I don't know what to say at this point, other than point out the fact that she definitely needs psychological help. I hold her, and she keeps saying

The Slender Man

"Don't leave me. Stay here," over and over again, as if begging me not to.

It breaks my heart when Dad comes up to tell me I have to. I hear the door open.

"Alright, let's go," he says.

"Dad I-"

"No."

"Dad listen-"

"Can it!" I feel his hand around my arm and he yanks me up. He really will drag me out even if I kick and scream. Before we leave the room, I look back at Shana and see that she's buried her head into her knees. She's crying now, and even I feel like I'm about to. It's not just because I'm sad to see her like this, but because I've seen weird things too, and I know something bad is about to happen.

The drive home is silent. I'm too busy worrying about Shana to say anything, and Dad is too busy not wanting to hear me complain to get me started.

When we get home, there is no Adam wandering the street. I guess having him go to sleep in Bubbe's room with his medicine did the trick. When we get inside, Dad tells me to get any homework I have left done, and then get to bed. I don't know why he emphasizes the homework. What homework I do have can all be done over the weekend, and since it's unlikely I'll be doing anything fun while being grounded, I'll have few distractions. Of course the distractions I have are huge. Like the strange things I'm seeing, the missing people, and most of all, Shana.

I'm not sleepy immediately, so after I'm in my pajamas-a plain tank top and sweat pants- I do as my dad said and work on my homework. No essays this week, but I do have a chemistry lab on Monday. We will be doing an experiment on... I don't even know. I flip open the book and try to find the pages that look like we went over most recently. I finally find a chapter on covalent bonding that looks familiar because of the pictures. I read over the chapter, but it takes me a while to cover it, because my mind keeps drifting off to Shana, and although my eyes are reading, my mind is worrying. Once I do finish the chapter I still have no idea what a covalent bond does, or even is.

I am starting to get drowsy from the stress and reading, but I decide to at least look over history. U.S history is a little easier. It's mostly about remembering names and dates, and if you get that right, A minus. As I read over the chapter the homework assignment is on, I think about Shana less. Maybe because social studies is less involved it's easier for your mind to stay on it. After reading a few pages though, my drowsiness kicks in and I lay my head down next to the book. I'm feeling lazy, but with my light on I'm not getting anywhere near sleep.

The Slender Man

I force myself to get up, push the book off my bed, and flick the light off. It's a little warm, so I only cover up with my top blanket. While lying down, I close my eyes to go to sleep. With my eyes closed and my mind sleepy I should be able to fall asleep quickly, but with a heart full of anguish and worry, I don't. As I replay the events of today over my head, I feel a few tears rolling down my cheek onto my pillow. From missing students, to failed essay, to Shana, whose only wish is for me to stay with her so she won't have to face Denise or "him" alone. I've succeeded in nothing today.

After a few more minutes, I feel that I am almost asleep, but then I hear wind rushing and open my eyes. I can't move. *It's happening again!* I think. I repeat the process of sending movement commands to my body, but this time I don't feel that slight twitch. Instead, I feel the static, or the numbing force that's holding me down pulse. It's like the more I fight, the stronger the force gets. Is he here? I look around with my eyes, probably the only part of my body I can move. I can sense him, but the room is empty.

Maybe he's going for Adam again? I can't see Adam in Bubbe's room across the hall, and even though I can't see the fiend, I know he's going for Adam now. Maybe if I wake up, I can get up. How do I wake up though? Last time I screamed myself awake. My lips are open just a bit, and I begin to push my voice out, but there's no sound. I try as hard as I can, to get that moan to come out, but there's nothing this time. It's as if he's stronger than before. I close my eyes. Maybe if I try to go to sleep, I will wake up? With my eyes closed, I try and drift into sleep, but then it hurts.

The static screeches and the grip tightens. I try to open my eyes, but I can't. No, am I locked in this blackness? I can still feel the bed pressing against me, but the static isn't letting up, and I can't even open my eyes. When I tried to drift into sleep, the grip tightened. Is this what Shana meant? Is this why she wouldn't go to sleep?

It is, she was fighting him! I have to too. I do everything I can to squirm, scream, and open my eyes. I feel my body trying to obey the commands from my brain, but his force won't relent. How long do I have to fight before he leaves? It feels like a minute; five; ten, but as I vainly fight I feel my heart racing, and my strength waning. Is he winning? I feel myself slipping... and then a tap.

I open my eyes and almost scream when I see something that looks like a shadowy hand disappearing underneath my bed. Not from around the bed, through it! I jump off the bed and hit the light switch in a single motion. I drop to the floor and look underneath the bed; nothing there.

"Adam," I mutter. I rush to Bubbe's room. Relief hits me as I see Adam in a pallet by her bed.

The Slender Man

He's breathing, and he's asleep. After splashing some water on my face, I walk back to my room. I consider falling back asleep. My body is tired, but what if that thing attacked, and won? I don't know what to make of it. Perhaps it was part nightmare, part real? I hope it's all nightmare and none of it is real, but I sleep with my light on just for the illusion of safety.

In what seems like only an hour, I feel hands pushing me. I violently jerk up and see my mother.

"Get up, something's wrong," she says. She hurries out of the room before I have a chance to respond. I hurry up behind her and my mind races. What could be wrong? Is it something to do with the static? Mom runs downstairs. I can see through the window that it's early morning. Adam was fine when I went to sleep, so unless he took him after the attack it wasn't him.

Maybe it left a message? I don't know what is happening, so I hurry downstairs as quickly as I can. When I get downstairs I'm surprised to see Mr. and Mrs. Hawthorn are standing there speaking with my Dad. When I come from around the stairway, they all look at me. Mrs. Hawthorn has tears in her eyes.

"Shana," I mutter to myself. Dad speaks first.

"Something's happened to Shana."

"Is she dead?" I ask horrified.

"We don't know," he answers.

"We were hoping she'd run away, and come here," explains Mr. Hawthorn.

"She's missing?" I ask. He nods.

All inside of a second, I feel a lump in my throat, my stomach gets heavy, and my heart begins pounding like a fist. I was right. I'd been right all along. Something bad was about to happen. Something bad did happen to Shana. Only when it did, I was worrying about Adam. Not once had it crossed my mind that the nightmare meant something was wrong with Shana. Maybe it's because the nightmare took place here that I assumed the fiend was after me or Adam.

I feel a hand touch my shoulder and look to see Bubbe standing beside me.

"Please, Alyssa. Did Shana say anything to you last night? You were the last person to have really spoken to her," asks Mrs. Hawthorn. I'm still not ready to answer. I'm not sure what to say. Shana's missing, like the other kids. Jason said he was going to help Kenny right after he saw the fiend, and then disappeared. That might have happened to the other missing students too. Shana saw Denise though, but instead of trying to help Denise, she stayed home, and wanted me to stay with her.

"She wanted me to stay," I finally say. "She, she didn't feel safe at home and wanted me to stay. She begged me." I'm saying this aloud for them to hear, but it sounds like I'm accusing myself.

The Slender Man

"I've just phoned the police. They're on their way," says Dad, who I didn't realize had left the room. I need to sit down, but I can't command my feet to move over to a chair, so I plop down onto the floor right where I am. My head hurts, and as I look around the room I can see I'm not the only one in pain. The Hawthorn's have already lost their youngest daughter, and they have only a shred of hope that they haven't permanently lost their first born daughter as well. As yet they have no reason to believe she's dead, but I know that she won't be found wandering the streets. I have to tell the police what Shana told me about Denise and *him*.

It's the only way I can help her, because even I don't have any clues as to how to help her any other way. She said that Denise wanted her to go help her in the forest, and that the *man* wanted her to sleep. Does going to sleep enable him to attack you? Does he put you in a trance and make you walk to him, or does he just whisk you away? I felt something trying to force me to go to sleep last night, but neither of those things happened, so what does it mean? Was the fit I had related to Shana's disappearance?

I sit here, thinking about what I could have done to prevent this. Maybe if I'd fought harder and stayed awake, Shana would be okay. Or maybe if I found a way to convince my Dad to let me stay she would be here now. If I hadn't turned in those essays I'd probably have been allowed to stay with Shana. I can't keep looking backwards though.

When I hear the knock on the door that can only mean the police are here I realize that the only thing I can do is try and help find her. I'm surprised to see that the sheriff personally came, and is accompanied by Deputy Yew, who looks utterly forlorn. He's stressed too. It's probably because he's been dealing with the other missing students, and now there is another one for him to find.

The sheriff begins by questioning the Hawthorn parents, and when they can't give him any information that might help, he comes to me. He doesn't have to say anything.

"When we visited on Thursday, she said she was seeing things. She said she was seeing her sister," I start.

"Like how you said Jason was looking for Kenny?" asks Deputy Yew from the corner. I nod, and continue on to explain how she said Denise wanted her help too, and that she couldn't go to sleep without seeing Denise. I tell them everything I can recall, including how Shana was refusing to fall asleep because she was afraid that *he* would get her. I almost sound crazy myself telling them this, but when I explain how Denise kept telling Shana to go to the woods, they finally look like I've given them a shred of decent information, other than the fact that Shana needed psychiatric help.

The Slender Man

"So if Shana gave in and tried to help her sister, her destination would be some point in the forest?" asks Sheriff Fraser, writing this down. I leave out the parts about how the apparition has also affected me and Adam, and how I suspect this is not as easy as Shana running into the woods.

"I think we need to issue a search party then. We can scan the entire forest," says the sheriff.

"If Shana went into the woods, there's a chance we might find the others too," he continues.

I look over his shoulder and see Mr. Hawthorn holding his wife, who's crying helplessly. "If we had known this, we'd have gotten her help immediately," he says. I don't believe that. If he really carried more about Shana's well-being than the shivah tradition, he'd have gotten her some help while she was catatonic, not wait until she disappeared.

I listen to myself. I listen to how hateful I sound. Being angry with her parents won't bring her back, but what will? Is there a chance that she really will be found in the woods along with the others? All I know is that there's a chance that this wouldn't have happened if I'd stayed with her in the first place. I keep thinking about the courses of action I could have taken to prevent being grounded: words I could have spoken; friendly gestures; not turning in the essays. It all leads to those essays. I feel a hand on my shoulder.

"We'll find your friend," says Deputy Yew. He's looking down at me with pity in his eyes. "Even if I have to do it myself," he adds. I'm surprised that he came to console me rather than her parents.

"We'll get to the bottom of this," throws in Sheriff Fraser.

"Alyssa," he says. I look at him.

"If anyone and I mean *anyone*, shows any signs of Shana's or Jason's behavior, you let us know immediately. I'm not sure what's going on, or why everyone's seeing things, but it all ties in with them going missing, and we can't have another disappearance on our hands," he explains.

I hesitate for a moment, trying to think of anyone that would confide in me about seeing the fiend, but even Jason only told me by chance.

"Will do," I say. The policemen take their leave, and I slump back down into the corner. I keep telling myself there's a chance they'll find her, but something inside tells me that's not going to happen. I've lost Shana, and I have no idea how to get her back. As the thought settles in, I feel heavy, and weak. I lay my head on my knees, mimicking the last position I saw Shana in, and feel her emptiness. I feel her sorrow, and I start to cry. It's all I can do. It's all I want to do. I'm sitting here like this for what seems like an eternity, before I feel another hand touch me. I look up and see the one person in the house who would try and comfort me in a time like this, Bubbe. My parents are with the Hawthorns and Adam is sick and in bed, but Bubbe sits down right beside me, arm around my neck. I smile and lean into her, like I would with Shana.

"Oh dear," she says. I look up and see her handing me a small hand towel. I first think it's because I'm crying, but as drops flow down the side of my lip I taste them, and I don't taste tears. I taste blood.

9: The Assembly

I feel less than human. I'm not sure if it's my emotions, or it's because of this new illness I've acquired. It's probably a combination of both. I'm walking into school, and every one of my limbs feels weighted. In my left hand I'm carrying a tissue to blot nosebleeds. My throat and nostrils both feel very dry, and my skin has paled from it. On the inside even my heart feels heavy with guilt, worry, and sadness. My actions are a factor in Shana's disappearance, and now that she's missing I can't stop thinking about her. All things considered, I feel like- like I'm dying. The medicine I'm taking doesn't work.

I'm thirsty no matter how much water I drink. It helps when I'm drinking it, but as soon as I swallow, the dryness returns. I feel like I've lost a pint of blood already. Nothing stops the nosebleeds that occur on and off several times per day. I can go a whole day without bleeding, and then have it run all night, and vice versa.

The police searched all Sunday for Shana. I remember seeing very many police cars, probably the whole force. I heard dogs barking, but the weeping of the Hawthorns, accompanied by my own, are what rings in my ears the most. They covered miles of woods- or so I'm told, yet Shana is nowhere to be found. The police finally began working with the press and are now hiring volunteer search parties to help cover more ground.

I can't believe my parents expect me to go to school like this. I feel worse than I've ever felt, and they haven't made Adam return to school, though of course his surgery is probably more of an excuse for prolonged absence. I was even expected to finish my homework, but every time I look at words on a piece of paper, my head throbs. It's not a headache, it's just- it's not the right time to be worrying about grades, even if I've fallen down to a C average. I worked on my homework, but I couldn't concentrate on the book well enough to find answers to the questions. I at least found the strength to Google the answers to the questions online. I know especially through recent events that cheating shouldn't even pop into my mind, but with everything going on it's the only way I'll get my work done. Plus-is it really cheating if I would have been looking up the answers in my book anyway? I consider Google more of a shortcut than a cheat.

As I walk into the school, I look around at everyone, but all of their faces seem blank to me. The only face I want to see is Shana's, and I'm worried that's a face I'll never see again. I slowly walk into English class, and catch a sympathetic look from Ms. Alder. I don't respect her sympathy. It may have been me that turned in those essays, but it's her that reported them. Because of that, I wasn't able to stay with Shana, and now she's missing. If she really sympathized with me, she wouldn't have reported me, or at least would have given me another week to do the essays on my own.

I sit at my desk and wait the few minutes for the bell to ring. I'm surprised when it does, because there are more than a couple of empty seats. One of course is Shana's, and another is Jason's, but it seems like someone else is missing, but with my mind almost shut down with worry, I can't name them. It's not like I know more than a few people in the class anyway.

Ms. Alder begins by having us open our literature books. Great, something I'll have to pay attention to. I am not the best at grammar, but so much of each lesson is redundant, and there are really only a few different grammar rules you learn in each one, like comma splicing. With literature I have to actually learn about poetry, or read stories. Those are subjects I won't be able to follow. I open the literature book and am reminded about our multicultural phase. I see words like "Haiku" and my mind just goes blank.

Ms. Alder always begins her lesson with her same monotonous teaching style. Sometimes I only get my cue to turn the page when the rest of the class does it. Other times I will glance over and see that my page looks completely different from another student's and quickly- but discreetly turn the page to match. I know Ms. Alder is probably keeping an eye on me and I don't want her telling my father that I'm not paying attention. I see drops of blood fall onto the pages and hold the tissue up to my nose. I accidentally inhale some of the fibers through my nose and they irritate my already dry and sensitive nostrils. I sneeze, and what looks like a full ounce of blood splatters onto not only the tissue, but all over my hand, and even more on the book. Of course Ms. Alder notices this.

"Oh Alyssa, go to the nurse immediately," she says.

"It's the same thing everyone else-"

"No, just go see the nurse. She might have something for you," she says.

I sigh and slam my book closed, hoping the blood seeps into more pages. It's not my book, and

I'm not the one who paid for it. She can lock this one up in that cluttered closet when I finish the school year- assuming I pass the grade. I walk out of the class, bloody tissue still in hand, and head down to the nurses office. There's nothing the nurse can give me that will work I'm just sick, and if I end up taking too many medications it will probably just put me in a worse condition.

I march down to the nurse's office, or at least I originally intend to, but come to think of it I've never been there, and I don't even know where it is. I walk almost aimlessly around the school's lobby trying to jar my brain to figure out where I might have seen it. I finally decide to head down toward the entrance near the offices when I see a sign that says "Nurse" and an arrow below it pointing into the hall. Now I recognize the place. The hall is actually just a corridor that leads to a shared sitting area for both the school nurse and the school counselor. The counselor has been justifiably absent this week, but I'm surprised that they haven't hired a substitute for her.

In the sitting area I see four students. Two of the students look just like me, another looks like he might be struggling with asthma, and the fourth looks just fine; he's probably just shamming. I decide that since I already know that the nurse can't do much about my nosebleed anyway, I'll just go patch it up myself. I leave the hall before anyone takes more than one good look at me and head down toward the restrooms. I get inside and can almost forgive Ms. Alder's adamancy. Blood is all over my hand and the lower part of my face. You'd think I have a raging case of hemophilia combined with a broken nose or something.

I think my body is reacting to the illness worse than the others. That makes sense given my poor immune system. I'm surprised it has taken me this long to catch it. I throw the soaked tissue away and begin rinsing my face with water. I watch as the blood dyes the water falling off my face. Once the water disappears down the drain, the sink shows only small signs of blood, I take a paper towel and plug my nose with it facing the ceiling. This usually hasn't worked for these nosebleeds so I guess I'm just doing this to feel like I'm doing something to combat the nosebleed at all. I feel a little bit of blood drain down the back of my throat and have to force myself to not cough and get blood all over the bathroom.

I hear the door open. I don't like the idea of people watching me handling a nosebleed or runny nose- or well, anything to do with my nose. Since tilting my head back isn't helping anyway, I decide I might as well go ahead and use the bathroom. I walk into the stall as the other person enters the restroom. I hear that the other person is in fact *two* people and they're talking to each other. I recognize the first voice as Lindsay Willow.

"...Yeah I was tardy today too. Mom wanted to work on my teeth. It's getting on my nerves because you're really only supposed to see the dentist like twice a year, but I already got my first check-up two months ago, and this is my second time. I think she's just bored 'cause she doesn't have many clients," she says.

"Yeah well my Mom didn't even want me to come today. You know another girl went missing? Well she says all of the missing people went crazy before disappearing, and she thinks I'm going crazy," says the other girl. I don't recognize her voice.

"Why would she think that?" asks Lindsay.

"Well I've been seeing things. Like I keep seeing this shadow out of the corner of my eye, and I keep having these real vivid nightmares about not being able to move and stuff like that. Hell, even I think I'm going crazy," laughs the girl. This is no laughing matter though.

I finish and leave the stall quickly.

"Do you see the static- the shadow in your nightmares?" I ask. Lindsay looks at me with a surprised look in her eye. Lindsay is Jason's age but she's in the grade above me. She has long black hair with blue streaks in it, and a small amount of bluish eyeliner around her blue eyes. You can tell her favorite color is blue. The other girl has a similar style except her hair is short and with orange streaks, and with her tan complexion looks like she's Filipino or Hawaiian. She's giving me a surprised look as well, as if I've startled her, but that surprise glides into a glare.

Lindsay speaks first. "You've got a little uh," she says, scratching under her nose. Oh right, my nosebleed.

"It's rude to listen into other people's conversations you know?" says the island girl. Great, instead of openly discussing it she just resorts to some snobby etiquette defense-mechanism. I roll my eyes and hold the tissue up to my nose.

"You want to bleed more?" she tests.

I look her in the eye. I'm not much of a fighter, especially now that I am sickened, but I would love to take my anger out on someone like her, and she's my size anyway *without* looking physically fit. I can take her. She and I stare each other down like a pair of angry dogs for a full ten seconds before Lindsay pulls on her arm. The girl gives me one more size-up before turning and following Lindsay from the restroom. As I wash my hands and try futilely to stem the blood flow, I hear a message over the intercom.

"Attention, at the end of this period, we need all students to be present in the auditorium. This is mandatory. Thank you," says Dad's voice. They're calling for a mandatory school assembly? The only time that happens is during graduation ceremonies, talent shows, plays, and things like that. This must have something to do with the missing students, or *him*?

No, even if the apparition is common news by now there would be no way it's discussed in public. Even people who have it would call the speaker crazy. I look at the clock on my phone. This period ends in three minutes. I decide I'll go ahead and walk to the auditorium since my class will already be heading there by the time I get back. When I get there I'm surprised that the place is already half filled. Some of the classes have already taken their seats and I even notice a couple pairs of parents. Maybe Dad spent the day summoning parents for this meeting. I see Ms. Alder has already started seating her students so I find myself a chair with the rest of my class. The seats are all blue folding chairs that aren't very comfortable, but I think they're in use for their mobility, because the auditorium is the room used for dances and parties. It's not long after I'm seated that the auditorium is full of students and staff. We end up waiting a few minutes before the guest speakers take their posts on stage. The speakers- are the police.

Several policemen including Deputy Yew and of course Sheriff Fraser take their places on stage.

The Slender Man

Deputy Yew stands uniformly with the other police, while the sheriff takes the stand.

"In all my time as sheriff this county has never seen much crime," he begins.

"The worst we've seen are a few cases of theft, and once, and only once, a murder that was promptly solved. So it fills me with deep regret to see that when tragedy strikes this county our police force seems to have no leads," he continues. He pauses before a brief moment, as if to collect his thoughts on how he's going to continue.

"Recently we lost more than ten of our dear children in a very tragic accident, and since then more of our children have disappeared," he says. There are no gasps of surprise from the audience. "We've been working on finding the missing children with no luck. Seven children have been reported missing since the accident. All of these children are affiliated with this school. I'm going to go over the list and if you've seen any of these children recently, please notify the police."

He begins to recite his list of students. He starts with Jason Larch and then moves onto the other students I haven't met.

"Shana Hawthorn...," he says, forcing me to wince. "...and most recently, Leanne Sourwood," he finishes. My eyes widen. Leanne is the other person I didn't see in class today. She must have gone missing over the weekend like Shana did. That means three of the missing children I know personally.

"Like I said we've narrowed the search down, and it seems they are all students in this school district. So we-"

"Have you found any suspects?" asks a voice. Sheriff Fraser looks around the audience to locate the voice, but I already know who it is before she stands up, Rita Larch. "Who are your suspects?" she repeats loudly. I use my hand- that's already working on stopping my nosebleed, to cover my face as I look down.

"Here she goes..."

"Well we've gathered some volunteers and our fine policemen are undergoing a thorough search of the surrounding forests," he says.

"Well what about Mario's house? Isn't he the number one suspect? Have you searched his house? Why are you searching the woods if you haven't searched through his house?" she banters.

"Now Mario Douglas is wanted for questioning since his disappearance from the hospital, but we have credible reason to believe that if these are kidnappings we are dealing with that he would be unable to commit them in his current physical state, and that he indeed may have been kidnapped as well," explains the sheriff.

"So? That doesn't make him innocent. I could kidnap a kid with a stubbed toe too," she argues.

"We will look into this, but we believe it is more likely a third party to-"

"Third party?" she interrupts. "Well who's the second party? Kids just don't go off missing on their own," she continues.

"Well we are also looking into the possibility that some of the first missing students- the ones that disappeared shortly *before* Mario did, may be partly responsible."

I wince. That is not the thing to say to Rita if you want her to shut up. She catches on to what he's saying, and I savor that brief pause she takes before she releases her outburst.

"How dare you accuse my son of- anything? I will find some real policemen and lawyers to put you down," she begins. As she continues shouting, I see Deputy Yew leave his position in the background and walk forward. He steps down from the podium and approaches Rita, who's sitting in the front row.

"Ma'am, I need to escort you from the audience," he says. I didn't see the sheriff issue a formal order or even wave, so the deputies must have received instruction to remove anyone who caused a scene. Whatever it is, the sheriff isn't objecting.

Rita sizes up Deputy Yew, who is only about her size. "Oh no, you have absolutely no right. In this country we have freedom of speech, and I will say what-" she protests, but he interrupts.

"Ma'am, in the country we also have laws against disturbing the peace. Now I'm going to ask you one more time to exit the building with me, or I will remove you from the premises by force."

I smile when I hear those words. If there is one good thing during all of this strife, it's hearing Rita Larch being put in her place. I can hear her objections as Yew escorts her through the hall, and then the sheriff resumes speaking.

"Like I said we have reason to believe that if these are kidnappings, that there is an unknown third party involved. Now we are doing all we can with our limited police force to put a stop to this. We've even notified the adjacent counties as well as the state police department," he finally says.

"Now one thing I have to say and another one of the main reasons I have brought you all here is that due to the multitude of students missing from this area, and the fact that an unknown third party is suspected to be responsible for their disappearances, the Cherokee County Board of Education has permitted a temporary district-wide suspension of educational activities," he announces, and you can tell he had to practice that one in the mirror.

Due to the grim situation, no one openly cheers, but I can see smiles cross the faces of many, even mine. It's not that I'm for skipping school, but with the losses I and those around me have suffered, I'm not fully able to focus on school.

"Are there any questions?" asks the sheriff.

"Yeah," says one parent, standing up.

"I understand the need for our children's safety, but how will we ensure the education of our children remains unaffected?" he asks. My smile fades.

"We've already worked this one out with the board, and we all agree that the teachers will issue a week's worth of their curriculum to be done at home. I understand that this still puts a dent in their education, particularly physical education and group functions, but I am not against meetings in private, supervised places and exercise at home. Our main priority is to keep the children of our community safe, and that's a lot easier to do when they're with their parents than at a school," he explains. I have to admit, aside from Rita, the sheriff knows how to plan ahead to give people what they want. Maybe that kind of leadership is why he's been elected.

"How long do you anticipate that this will take?" asks another parent.

"We are hoping to solve this issue immediately, but hoping to and doing so are two different things. To ensure operational security, will be giving limited updates to the public, but if we find any priority suspects, or any of the children, we will let you know," he answers. A few more parents ask random and sometimes redundant questions, but the sheriff eventually closes the school assembly with one final note.

"One more thing I'd like to add is, people close to the missing children noted that shortly before the child disappeared, they complained of hallucinations. If anyone has hallucinations about seeing missing relatives, please notify the police, as that may something to do with their disappearances. Thank you." After saying that, he steps off the podium and leaves the crowd to be excited and somewhat bewildered. I can see why he would wait to say that until after the barrage of questions were answered. After all, even I'm seeing things.

10: The Reprieve

I can't seem to get any sleep. Whenever I try to rest I end up with my face buried in a pillow; sleepy but not sleeping. You'd think that with my health and all of the drama going around that sleep would be the perfect escape, but I just can't seem to reach it. I lay here on my bed listening to the sound of dishes clanging as breakfast is being made. When I feel blood running down from my nose again, I have to force myself to get up and take care of it. I grab a tissue from the box that's been lying on my bed all night. I wipe up the blood and then throw the tissue in the trash can that has been sitting beside my bed all night as well. By now you can see nothing but bloody tissues inside.

I come up to a sitting position and take in just how gross I feel. Well, not necessarily gross, but the dryness isn't just in my throat and nose now. Now I feel like it has spread to my skin and I'm getting even worse. I sluggishly walk downstairs to get breakfast, maybe that will help. Mom has made muffins and eggs. When she sees I've entered the kitchen she begins fixing me a plate. I grab the carton of orange juice from the refrigerator and pour myself a hefty glass. I'll have enough Vitamin C to last a week. Mom sets my plate on the table and I sit down. Adam is in the chair next to me and he's already eating. He looks like he's fully recovered from the crash, aside from his broken arm, but I can tell he looks just as sickly as I do. One thing I notice about him is that he's all dressed up.

"Are you feeling any better Lyss?" asks Mom. I shake my head after taking a big gulp of orange juice so my throat is clear enough to answer.

"I feel worse," I say.

"Have you taken your medicine?" she asks. "Yes," I lie. The last medicine I've had is Nyquil, and I'm supposed to be taking some antihistamine tablets as well, but they don't do any good. In fact, the antihistamine makes me feel more dried out. As I eat, I feel some buildup around my labret and notice that blotches of dried blood have clotted around it.

"Maybe you should fight through it?" Mom suggests.

The Slender Man

"What do you mean by that?" I ask, mouth full of eggs.

"You don't have school today. Why don't you go out and exercise? You know? Power through it?" she explains. Exercise would be the last thing to cross my mind at a time like this, but I ponder it and the cardio at least would help get my mind off things. Heck it might even help me get to sleep.

"Yeah I'll go for a run," I finally answer.

"Oh, but not before finishing your schoolwork, I don't want you to get your work piled up at the end of the week," she adds. Correction, schoolwork would be the last thing to cross my mind at a time like this.

"Alright," I sigh. After breakfast I head upstairs to wash my face. I use cold water and follow up by slathering on lotion to try to help the uncomfortable dry feeling. I notice that the area under my nose is cracked and irritated from all the tissues. I really wish we had some of those lotion-enhanced tissues or whatever they're called. I notice that my complexion isn't the only thing that looks out of sorts. My hair is a mess and even my nails need work. It may not be the time for vanity but I do take pride in my appearance, and I don't want to end up looking like a crazy old hag. I brush my hair out thoroughly and work on getting it into a ponytail since I'll be running later. I decide not to worry about makeup since I'll be showering off after I run anyway.

Today is Tuesday, which means Lionel Willow's birthday party is today, so I need to look... sane. I get dressed in some warm weather exercise gear; in fact I choose almost the same outfit I wore out on my last run with Shana. After dressing I open my backpack to look at the bulging folder of homework. I didn't bother organizing them when I received the papers. All the teachers really gave us were instructions to read a set amount of chapters, and then the homework for each chapter. I decide rather than going one day at a time, I'll go one subject at a time.

I'm feeling tired so I am not in any mood to try and memorize anything. I start with algebra. Many people complain that algebra is hard but the truth is, all you have to do is remember the formula and then answer the questions using the formula that's right there in front of you. I can do it almost absentmindedly.

As I work through each problem I force myself not to think about Shana because it will only distract me. Every time the name "Shana" pops into my head I think of random words until I'm back on track. With my mind bouncing around with phrases like 'pie' and 'I just ate' fluttering through my mind I get my homework done a little more slowly than I'm used to, but it's the most progress I've made in any kind of work since the accident, and when I'm finished a little smile crosses my lips.

"Productivity," I say to myself, and on that note, it's time to be even more productive and get some exercise. Let's fight this sickness, as my mom put it. I keep mentally reassuring myself that I can do this. I won't have to jog the whole course. Maybe because I'm sick, I'll do intervals of walking and jogging. I make sure to bring a full bottle of water to prevent dehydration. I'm sure I can persevere, and my only real worry is that my nose will bleed uncontrollably so I carry plenty of tissue in my backpack.

I head out the door and start into a slow jog, but immediately I feel the leaden weight brought on by my sickness and I find myself jogging at the average speed of a brisk walk. I stare at the ground watching the white cement sidewalk pass by. This way I don't pay too much attention to just how slow I am really moving. When I see the shadow of the stop sign I look up at the tree line. *Am I going to be able to handle this?* I think as I already feel tiny beads of sweat on my clammy hands. I do some brief stretches just in case. If there's any bad time to twist an ankle, it's when you're sick and haunted by a ghastly static apparition.

After a few stretches I look both ways and take off. I throw my knees forward to carry my weight through. I hit the tree line and descend into the forest. I try to ignore my dry throat as I stomp through fallen leaves that have covered the whole ground at this point. I look around at the trees while I'm running. Most of them have been stripped bare at this point. Now all of the once beautiful trees are naked and gloomy. It looks normal in late autumn but at this time of year they just seem off. Is it the season or the current events making this seem so strange?

By the time I reach that first true incline I'm walking. I don't have the strength to run up the hill this time. I'm already sweating pretty badly and am constantly wiping my eyes on my jacket sleeve to stop the sweat from burning my eyes.

I'm grateful that my nose isn't bleeding right now otherwise I might have just gotten blood all over my favorite hoodie. When I reach the top of the hill, I find it's harder to throw my knees forward again. I've heard that for cross country runners the trick is to not stop running. I use that little bit to motivate me to press forward once more.

I feel weaker now, like the resting pace and water didn't rejuvenate me at all, and keep getting the idea to just call it a day. *No, I came out here to fight this. Let's finish the whole course. I won't let this illness run my life,* I think to myself. I keep using those thoughts to motivate me, and hope to God that I don't stop running and then not have the energy to start up. Sweat keeps pouring into my eyes- well my right eye. I am constantly forcing my right eye shut, only looking with my left. I should really invest in a head band. I keep running on and finally reach that last slope that marks the clearing. I'm going to sprint this one. Each bound takes a severe toll on my strength and by the time I reach the hill I have to bend over to catch my breath. "Head above the heart. Always keep moving," I say to myself. I put my hands on my hips to keep my back straight and walk in a circle around the clearing.

I realize I'm circling that strange tree. I stop and look up at it. It seems a little taller than before. If I'd remembered the scare this tree gave me last time, I probably wouldn't have been able to motivate myself to come out here again. I am about to look away from the tree when something catches my eye; the branches. I remember last time there were how many branches, five or six? I count them this time.

"Nine," I say aloud. It has those two jointed branches hanging toward the ground like before, but seven of them are angled up. I only remember four branches angled up last time. Trees don't just sprout new branches like this. It's eerie to see this. I may be no good at memorizing schoolwork, but when a strange tree appears full grown on my jogging route and then sprouts new branches suddenly I tend to take a mental note. There are nine branches on this tree. I repeat that thought aloud too. Next time I come on my run I'm going to count the branches again.

I shake out my limbs, rotating my neck and ankles for the home stretch. I am about to descend when I remember what happened last time. I thought I'd seen the entity, but it was just the tree. Or was it the fiend after all? Now I feel uncertain and a shiver runs through me. Now I'm just scaring myself. Maybe I should sprint back like last time? No, that would have been impossible for me to do if I hadn't thought I was about to die in the woods. I'm just going to run, and I'm not going to look back at the tree this time. I bite the back end of my labret, and then I'm off. I run a little faster than I did on the way here, but I think it's a pace I can sustain. I'm going to conquer this. I keep running, far past the clearing, but that level of fear I had last time keeps creeping up on me.

I start seeing things out of the corner of my eye. It's like my mind is purposely trying to scare me. It's showing me the fiend, except not as vivid as it usually does. Then I see *him* again. He's far in front of me this time, but as I clear more trees he disappears again. Then he reappears. It's as if I'm following him, except I'm only catching glimpses.

Surprisingly, my fear recedes, as if I'm not really scared. Good, I think. There's something off about the way I keep catching him. First, I see this dark spot past a small tree ten meters from me. Then, it's the same thing fifteen meters. Now I can hardly see him. Maybe he really is here. Is he moving? If he is, then why isn't he coming for me? The fear begins to rise again. What if he *does* come for me? He's ahead of me so I would be easy to intercept. I detour around, trying to move in an angle on the way home. I can't see him anymore.

I trip and face-plant myself into ground. The leaves cushion my fall, but in my condition, getting up isn't so fun. I push myself off the ground and see a few drops of blood. Great, the collision triggered my nosebleed. I reach into my pack and pull out some tissue. I look around the area and don't recognize it. I'm not really lost though, and I walk east until I see the end of the tree line. I emerge onto the road. I look at the paved road boarded by the forest that leads south to my home neighborhood. I walk toward my neighborhood, which is only a kilometer or so away when a thought dawns on me. Why would he be going directly ahead of me, unless it was trying to beat me to my destination? "Adam."

My feet are running faster than I tell them to. The first time I saw the static shadow he was looming over Adam. Does that mean he's finally come to collect him? I feel weakened already from the exercise mixed with the sickness, and the lag I'm suffering only increases my worry. I have to get home! My feet thud against the ground and it feels like I'm kicking through molasses to move them forward. When I finally get to my front door, it's ajar. "Adam!" I call. I run upstairs, the loud thuds of my footsteps blocking out the sound of the creaking floorboards. I go to his room, empty.

"Adam!" I call again. I check Bubbe's room, empty also. I run downstairs and see that no one is present.

"Mom?" I call. Worry sets in further. Would it take both Adam and my mother? I hear a noise. It's faint at first but then I realize just how close it is. I turn around, but the sound is still behind me. I listen again. It's coming from my backpack. It's my cell phone vibrating. I remove my backpack and open it. I look at my phone and see that I've received a text from Mom. I read it.

"Went to the party early with Adam help set up. Dad and Bubbe went to get Lionel's present and have it wrapped. They will be there to pick you up soon, bring the camera. It's on the kitchen counter." A wave of relief sets in. All this stress, worry, and relief can't be good for my health, I think.

I look at the time. It's a little after one-thirty and the party starts at three, so I have plenty of time. I head upstairs and drop my backpack onto the rest of the mess on the floor. I kick my shoes off in random directions and yank out my ponytail. I grab a few toiletries and head to take a shower. I turn the water on and while the temperature is moderating I take a look in the mirror. I grimace at what I see. I know the sun isn't too bright but I'd hoped I'd at least have a little more color in my skin after the run to hide just how sick I am. I remove my clothing, and after I see steam rising from behind our translucent shower curtain I stick my hand in to test the water, making sure it's not too hot.

I get inside, but instead of immediately washing off I lie down as if I were taking a bath, letting the hot water rinse the sweat and other ickiness off my skin. I almost don't feel up for a party after that run, but I think it's mutually understood that something small like a child's birthday party will help liven up everyone's mood, even if just a little.

After what feels like ten or fifteen minutes I force myself to get up and wash before the hot water runs out. By the time I turn the water off, my skin already feels dried up. I apply some lotion and change into the day clothes I brought with me. I have a green, Happy Bunny tank top as an undershirt, and I put on my green and black flannel shirt over it. I figure the blouse will match the nail polish, even though it's pretty badly worn out by now. I put on deep blue jeans and green socks. After my clothes are on, it's time to work with my wet hair. I use the toilet as a chair and then grab our blow dryer. It's pretty out of date: old; bulky, and black, but it works. I dry out my hair then brush it out. It's still a little damp when I'm finished, but acceptable.

I exit the bathroom, leaving my clothes on the floor where I took them off- I'll pick them up later. I throw on some thin rubber bracelets on my left arm. I use black and blue, because I don't have green ones, but I do have a black and green Yeah Yeah Yeah's bracelet that I put on my right arm. I apply a little eyeliner and lip gloss and take one good look at myself in my vanity mirror. I need to bleach my hair again, as my roots are showing pretty badly, but other than that I look... normal.

I let out a little sigh. It's not really audible, but my body goes through the motions. Ever since the accident I haven't really been myself, and to see how much damage the recent tragedies have done to my appearance only makes me feel worse. I look up at the framed picture of Shana and me from two years ago. We were standing outside our school, facetiously making duck faces, and wearing matching blue and silver halter top dresses for the school dance.

"If only you were here now," I say. I touch the frame, only now noticing that a thin layer of dust has built up on it.

"Where are you?"

11: The Party

I fumble around with the camera while we're in the car. It's not a very new camera, in fact I think my parents have had it for a decade at least, but it works. It's rather bulky, so my parents only bring it on special occasions. Like Hanukkah, the Fourth of July, and well- birthday parties. It's big and black, and the lens-holder thingy takes up more than half of it. It's got a grip for holding it, but I am just wearing it around my neck. Dad just picked me up from the house and now we're driving to the party. Bubbe is staying at home. I guess she's not very interested in going to a children's birthday party. I look out the window. The drive to the Willow's house isn't particularly far, in fact it's only a few miles from ours, but it's one of those places set up a mile away from any other building. Everything else is just tree line.

When we pull up to their house, which is very big compared to our house, I see quite a few people have already shown up. In fact it looks like the party has been going on for a while now. It's taking place in their enormous front yard, and they even pitched large tan canvas tents up to provide some shade. Dad pulls up and Karen Willow waves to catch our attention. Dad stops the car and rolls the window down.

Karen walks up with a big smile. "Hi! We were wondering when you two would make it," she greets.

Dad gives her a polite little laugh and smile as a response. "Glad to be here. Hey where do you want us to park?" he asks.

"Oh, we're having all the cars pull around the other side here. Just find a spot, but make it look neat," she answers. Dad gives her a little nod as she backs off. As we reach the other side of the yard some dozen cars or so come into view, though they aren't parked very neatly. It seems that the general idea is to park them side by side facing the tree line. That works for us though, so Dad pulls up to the end of the car-line and parks. I hop out and open the back door.

Dad picked up Lionel's present on his way back. It's a jumbo Captain America shield, hidden in a cheap gift bag. Part of the shield actually sticks out, but the visible part is covered in gift wrap. Behind the present is a twenty-four pack of Mountain Dew- Dad can carry that. I walk to the party, gift in hand, hoping that this party will bring more merriment than kids birthday parties usually do for me. I feel that it won't though, because every birthday party I've gone to here, whether mine or someone else's, has been with Shana. It will be awkward not having her here, but if I can just keep my mind off of her, maybe it won't be so bad.

I reach the others and Karen, who was already walking toward us, takes the present and guides me into the house. I guess she doesn't want Lionel to know he has gifts today. She leads me across her white wooden porch into her house. The inside of her house isn't as green and white as the outside though. It's surprisingly very empty. I mean, it has everything normal houses would, like bookshelves, couches, a TV and whatnot, but it's missing decorations. There are no paintings or trinkets, grandfather clocks or throw rugs, or anything. The most you will find in this living room are some family portraits set about on end tables- excuse me, *the* end table. I guess the Willows aren't very frivolous people, but then again, maybe it's just that we are in comparison. In our living room you'll find over a dozen candles and framed pictures of the "art" Adam and I created when we were little. Not to mention Stars of David and Judaica.

She leads me through the living room to a door at the base of her stairs. It's a small coat closet. There are many gifts in the closet, both wrapped and unwrapped, and ours fit in nicely with the others.

"Thank you guys so much for coming. I was worried you guys wouldn't want to, especially with what happened to Shana," she says. I can tell she's trying to appear grateful, but reminding me of Shana won't do that. God, every time I hear her name there's a lump of guilt, worry, and a few other nasty emotions, and the more I feel it the less it wants to go away.

"Oh, wouldn't miss it for the world," I answer.

"Help yourself to some cupcakes and ice cream. We haven't brought out the big cake yet, and to be honest it's mostly just for dunking his face in," she says, following up with a loud and annoying low-pitched laugh.

"Thanks, I will,"

"They're out under one of the tents," she says. I leave the house and go straight to it. I haven't eaten since breakfast, and although it's hard to choke food down with my throat being dry, I need to get something in my stomach, especially chocolate- lots and lots of chocolate. Underneath the canvas tent is a table covered in a white sheet being used as a tablecloth. The cupcakes are all red white and blue with little Captain America rings on them. I hate when they do that. Why can't the rings just be in the box, not in the cupcakes? Every time I try and pull a ring out of a cupcake (except for those thin little Halloween spider ones) I end up taking half of the frosting with it, and I don't like licking the frosting off the ring. It makes me feel like a pig. I search around for the chocolate ones and am disappointed to find that they are all vanilla. Except, wait, is that marble? I pick up one of the cupcakes and pull the wrapped down a bit. Awesome, they bought marble cupcakes as well. These will have to do.

I look around the table and see that there are also chips, beverages, and Neapolitan ice cream. There are also mini Captain America plates and plain white utensils. Doesn't anyone bring serve food at birthday parties anymore? I set the cupcake down on a plate and pick of a can of tea. I turn around and see Mom coming under the tent with an empty plate, which reminds me.

"Here Mom, I brought the camera," I say, pointing to the twenty pound rock hanging from my neck.

"Oh good, will you take pictures?" she asks. I pause for a moment. I have to take pictures now? If I'd known I would be asked to do this I would have conveniently forgotten the camera on the table or something. I sigh quietly as I find a good place to eat my cupcake. The Willows have some tables set up. There are actually a lot of tables, around ten or so, and each seats six, far too many for the amount of guests. Who all did they expect to come, the entire county? I find an empty table. It's a habit of mine to find the least occupied table, but the habit isn't drawn from not liking the others, I simply had a better person to converse with. I shake my head, hair flying into my face, before that name pops into my head.

It's too late though as I feel that lump in my chest again. I sit down at the table and gloomily eat my cupcake- or at least half of it, but my appetite is gone. I look at the half eaten cupcake. I pick up the bulky camera and take a picture of it. *Here you go Mom, you can upload this to your Facebook.* The cupcake has dried out my throat a bit, so I open the tea and sip it. My face cringes when I find out it's diet. Who feels the need to make diet tea, much less pay for it? Ugh.

I can taste the aspartame or whatever it is they use to make good drinks taste like crap and call it diet, and suddenly have the desire to finish my cupcake. When I do I wipe the crumbs off my hands and gather my plate and napkin. I walk around a bit, looking around at the attendees. There are less than twenty, which is strange for the dozen parked cars. I begin to think that maybe most of the guests were lone visitors that came just out of courtesy. Couldn't bring their little ones along too- oh right.

I spot a trashcan near the food tent and am on my way when I see the birthday boy. He's walking in my direction, wearing a big Captain America shirt, Captain America party hat, Capt- well they should have just put him in a Captain America costume. I approach him and crouch down to his level. "Hey there Lionel, having fun?" I ask. He looks me in the eye, and I don't see happiness, I see fear. Is he scared of me? He's still pretty pale from the sickness, so maybe that's putting him off. I'm barely handling it. I can only imagine how a five year old would. "You're five now! Are you excited?" I ask.

He gives me a half-smile. It's like he knows this is a time for him to be happy, and like me, he's trying, but also like me it's not working so well. "Smile!" I say, trying again. I hold up the camera and take a picture of him. He's not smiling in the picture, but he's not frowning either. Instead he's giving the camera a pretty blank look. We can caption it something nice like *curiosity* or *wonder*.

"Lionel," I hear Adam call. Lionel looks over. Adam approaches from behind with a few signatures on his cast. Not many kids here. I think maybe they're from overly-enthusiastic adults trying to be courteous.

"Your Mom wants you. They're setting up the piñata," he says. Oh, a piñata. That's something Mom will want pictures of.

Adam takes the ever-so-quiet Lionel by the hand and guides him to the game. I follow, getting a little annoyed by the slow pace of small children, but distract myself by snapping pictures of random, pointless things that no one is going to remember. I mean who needs a picture of guests lounging around, some holding cans of soda, and others looking like they're ready to go already? I sure don't.

They're setting up the piñata around the side of the house on a small cherry tree. The tree is so out of place that I have no doubt that it was planted by the Willows to honor some family event. I'm surprised that the piñata has nothing to do with Captain America. It's a Batman Symbol. Maybe it was brought by one of the guests, or maybe the party supply shop was all out of Captain America ones. I take a few more pictures of them setting up it up, and then finally a pretty good one of Lionel wearing a red blindfold and holding a wooden stick. Lionel hesitates for a while, as if he's really not interested in the piñata, but finally after a little goading he starts swinging. He misses again and again, but when he finally does hit it he doesn't leave a dent or even a scratch. He gets the idea of where it is though, and begins repeatedly bashing it, but he's still not getting it. I take some shots of him swinging at it though.

After I get a few, I decide any more would be too redundant and take a look at the ones I have. They're coming out pretty well. *I should be a photographer.* Conveniently, it is decided that Lionel has run out of turns (at a count of well over thirty) and it's one of the other kids' turns. The other kids are only Adam and some other girl that looks like she may be related to Rita's friend, the scene girl I almost got in a fight with. They decide to let the girl go first, and I catch some photos of her, and then they let Adam go. Adam is at a disadvantage with a broken left arm, but at least he's right handed. When he's ready, he takes a powerful full width swing that causes spectators to back up. The swing knocks the piñata back and forth, causing Adam to miss his next few tries, but when he does hit it, it comes to the ground. Wow, only two swings. I'm not sure if it was because the piñata was weakened or if he really is that strong with one arm.

I suddenly realize that I forgot to take any photos of Adam swinging the piñata. I shake my head a bit. It's no big deal. I'll just get one now while Adam is still standing there with a hint of triumph over his mournful demeanor. I point the camera and shoot. When the shutter opens again, I see something in the distance. It's not too far away, maybe fifty feet or so. I zoom in and recognize it. I see *him*.

Is he moving at all? Is he getting closer to us? I instinctively snap a picture. I move the camera away from my face and look with my eyes. I can definitely see a shadowy figure but my eyes get fuzzy and start to sting when I stare at him. Would he just approach us at the party like this? I walk forward to get a better look, but the stinging comes up again, forcing me to close my eyes.

It doesn't look like he is moving though. It's as if he's just standing there, just before the tree line; watching. I point the camera and zoom in again. Through the camera I can see pretty okay but my eyes still sting. It's good that he's not approaching us. Maybe he's worried that he'll get caught if he tries to snatch someone with this many people in the area.

That being said, I'm still getting pretty shaken looking at him. He's not just some shadow that moves like static. It's more like he's an outline *made* of shadow or something; a silhouette. I want a good look at him but that strange discomforting feeling burns my eyes whenever I try to look.

Well, the closest I can come to describing the sensation is that it feels exactly like the time Shana and I read online that you can simulate being high by forcing your eyes to stay wide open while rolling them up into your head as hard as you can and keeping them that way for as long as you can. Try it and you will know just how horrible it feels to try to look at this creature.

His body doesn't appear to have a definite shape and it's even more difficult to it make out because of the pain in my eyes, but I think I can make out- a humanoid figure? He can't be human can he? *He* is actually a man? No, he seems way too tall for that. He doesn't exactly rival the trees, but this thing's shape, appearance, and movements look like something out of a Marilyn Manson video.

I zoom in closer, causing my eyes to sting again. I force just one to open to look. He's one hundred percent black and what appear to be his arms come down almost to the ground. It looks like he's just standing there and is perfectly still aside from the violent static-shaking. I can't make out any features, but one distinct thing I notice about him is that something appears to be protruding from his back. I think they're tendrils of some sort. I try to look closer but the stinging becomes unbearable. I can't tell what this entity is supposed to be, but if anything, he isn't natural. I snap a photo.

This isn't right. I never doubted anything paranormal was in play here. Whether he's a ghost or a specter or something like that, I always knew I was really seeing something. I take another. Now that I'm seeing him though, now that I'm watching him... watch us, I feel a drop in morale. Is this what took Shana, Jason, and the others? Is this... thing... coming for me too? I can't let just let him stand there. I have the urge to yell and send the others rushing over to attack him. The Willows have a gun right? Who in this town doesn't? Even my Dad keeps a twelve-gauge that I'm only supposed to touch if there's someone breaking in.

No, I know the game. If I panic, he goes poof, and people will think I'm crazy. I won't be the crazy one. I do my best to seem like I am taking pictures of the children, so he won't see me noticing him. I think of a better idea.

"Hey!" I call in no particular direction, but I look around to find the perfect person. I catch the eye of one of the men. It's Jamie Willow, Lionel's father. I think he's a postal worker, or no, maybe a teacher for the elementary school. I think I've seen him once when I picked Adam up at school before, but I'm not sure. All I know is that he's trying too hard to look like he's still in his twenties.

"Hey you're the Redwood kid right?" he asks.

"Um, yeah, hey listen. This may be nothing, but I think I saw someone in the woods over there watching the kids," I say, keeping an eye on the shadow-figure to make sure he's still looming around over there.

"You sure?" he asks. Wow, this guy is pretty dumb for a teacher, maybe he is just a postal worker, or maybe he doesn't feel like looking.

The Slender Man

"Well, I'm not a hundred percent positive it's a person, but I saw something over there. Will you check it out? Again it's probably nothing, but with all of the missing kids and this being a kid's birthday party and all," I say.

He nods a bit, following my gaze to the trees. "Yeah okay," he says reluctantly. I guess his chivalry trumped his need to linger around the highlight event of a dying party.

"What's going on Lyss?" Mom asks from behind.

"Oh I just asked Jamie over there to check something out for me," I say.

Mom gets that look on her face she gets when she hears what I say but it doesn't really make sense to her, you know, with her brows knitted and one corner of her mouth raised in a subconscious shadow of a sneer.

"Huh, well hey have you gotten any good photos yet?" she asks. *The photos! Of course. She will be able to see the static-creature too!* I eagerly yank the camera off my neck and hand it to her, but not before pressing the review button.

She looks at the photo and doesn't just flip through it like I half expected her to. I look over toward Jamie and see that the entity is still there, and he's getting closer. Wait a second, what if that fiend attacks him? Will I have just sent a man to his untimely death? Then again, shouldn't he see that dark fiend by now? I'm seeing him from over here, does that mean- "What's wrong with the camera?" she asks.

I look back over. "What do you mean? It's fine," I answer.

"No, these photos are all distorted...oh no these ones are fine," she says. I snatch the camera from her.

"Hey, what is the matter with you?" I look at the monitor. She's on the photo I took of Lionel before the piñata; it looks fine. I flip through, looking at all the photos I've already seen until I get to it, the one of the monster. It's been blurred and blackened, as if someone damaged the screen. I'm beginning to feel like I am stuck in a cheesy, overdone psychological thriller movie.

I feel a push against my shoulder. "Answer me! What is with your attitude? I've been nothing but nice to you," she continues.

"Oh, I'm sorry- I didn't mean to. I didn't break the camera," I finally say.

"Well, I didn't say you broke it, you just had the dial turned to the wrong setting or your finger must have been in the way is all. Just be more polite. God knows your father wouldn't have tolerated that," she says.

"Take some more pictures though," she adds.

I nod my head once while turning to look back at the man. "Yes ma'am."

The Slender Man

Jamie is out of sight, but the fiend is still there. Did he eat Jamie or something? No wait, there's Jamie. He's like ten feet into the forest, well past the monster. What's he doing? How would he walk right through him, unless... Jamie couldn't see him? Did the fiend just not touch him? Maybe I really am seeing things or it is just a tree? No, even hallucinations aren't supposed to- the fiend is moving. He's not walking, but he's clearly turning. My eyes sting, but I watch as he hunches over and leans forward, turning his head and seeming to refocus his eyeless gaze. He's found what he was looking for-a new target. He's looking at me.

The burning in my eyes suddenly becomes overwhelming and I flinch, waiting for something to happen, but nothing does. Jamie returns with an annoyed look and gives me a little shrug, like I'm just some paranoid little girl making up stories for attention-

The feeling of being in a low-budget film increases. I can finally sympathize with those female characters I always found so annoyingly stupid. Of course you can't just run for help, people will just think you're crazy. I know what I see right now. It's not my fault Jamie can walk right through the shadowy monster. I try to ignore the entity, but now I fear I've caught his attention. It can't be just because I noticed him can it? Lots of people have noticed him, or something like him. Then again, everyone I know that has noticed him is now missing. Does this mean it's my turn?

Some of my Bubbe's advice rings in my ears. She has always told me to be strong, and not let anyone or anything bother me. That's just what I'll do. I look away from him and rejoin the party. It looks like the candy has already been claimed by the few present children, but I snap a few shots anyway- after deleting the damaged ones I took of the fiend. How did those ones end up getting messed up? Is it that static I hear when he's near; does it cause interference? I know when I looked at him my eyes stung and I had to look away, so does that mean he has a similar effect on the camera? I shake my head. I need to just not worry about it. If Jamie was okay after walking right through him, the least I can do is ignore him right?

It looks like the Willows are bringing out the cake. This means one thing, the party has reached its climax. They are gonna sing happy birthday, slam Lionel's face into the cake, open presents, and then we leave. The sooner the better, because then we can get away from the stalking entity over- he's gone. No, he's not gone, he must have just moved because I can still... feel him... I realize I've sensed him since we got here, an almost audible static noise running under everything. I hear everyone singing Happy Birthday and realize I must have spaced a good few seconds. I join in, although rather quietly.

I'm suddenly glad I decided to not bring my guitar, because it feels like my singing voice has gotten worse due to the sickness. As we sing, Karen Willow brings out the -of course- Captain America birthday cake for Lionel. It's got a candle shaped into the number five burning on top of it. It's actually rather small, but I can see her husband Jamie carrying a larger cake behind her. That must be the one for the guests. She sets the cake on the table and gets Lionel to blow out the single flame. I take a shot of that and then I catch the next scene when Karen forces Lionel's face into the cake. His face smashes the cake into a giant mush with only some of the outer edges intact.

Lionel jerks his face out of the cake, not fully certain what just happened, and examines it. He's silent for a few seconds but then he slowly but steadily begins crying. I feel a little guilt wafting in as I watch Lionel, face completely covered in icing and cake, mourn the tragic destruction of the treat he was so excited for. I snap a photo of it, and hope that in time he'll look back and laugh at himself. I hate seeing little children cry, even just Adam's recent subdued persona brings me down. I can only imagine what it was like for him.

As bad as I feel with Adam being hurt and my best friend missing, he actually was physically hurt and had to watch as his best friend and classmates died, and he's half my age!

Karen calms Lionel down a bit but he's still quietly sobbing. He finally takes a bit of the destroyed cake as Jamie dishes out pieces of the large plain white cake to everyone else. I don't take a piece though. The cupcake was enough for me.

As the cake is being eaten, Lindsay and Jamie haul out the various gifts for Lionel to claim. At this point he's excited again, or maybe excited for the first time. I haven't seen him really fully smile during the whole party. The first present he opens is a very small one, but pretty expensive- a small handheld game console. It's one of those educational ones. Next he opens our gift, his big plastic shield. His eyes light up when he sees what it is, and his reaction even causes me to smile. That's something worth capturing on camera. His other gifts consist of learning-to-read books, a remote control monster truck, and things like that. His parents got him a Captain America costume, which matches perfectly with the shield. Maybe our parents collaborated on that one.

As I predicted, once the gifts have been given, the party begins to die out. Of course, we're some of the last ones to leave. In fact, Mom wants to stay and help clean up. Karen gave her a ride here, so we can't just leave her, which means the only way for us to go home any time soon is for Dad and me to help. I begin gathering cups, plates, and cans that were left lying around the place. Did no one but me notice the big trash can that was provided? I pile it all into the one trash can, getting as much into the overflowing bag as I can, before Dad gets the bright idea to hand me an empty trash bag to carry around. Smart me.

I feel a little tension release as I clean up. I realize that it is because the background static that was setting my teeth on edge is gone. I look around. Is that monster still here? No, I can't see him. He must have left, finally. I take a deep relaxed breath and continue my job. Dad hauls both trash bags over to the dumpsters, and then begins to work with Jamie on getting the tables, chairs, and tents put away. Mom's idea of helping is to stand at the front door chatting away with Karen while the three of us do the work. I guess since she came and helped earlier with the set-up, she doesn't feel the need to help now, which sounds fair assuming it wasn't just Lindsay, Jamie, and some of the other guests that set things up while she chatted with Karen. Where is Lindsay anyway, and why isn't she helping? She must be inside with Lionel.

I help Dad and Jamie by picking up plastic chairs and carrying it out to the storage shed where they're storing the other items. I keep an eye out for the fiend, making sure he's not about to ambush me or anything, but there's no sign of him. When everything including the canvas and poles for the tent are piled in the garage, the yard looks strangely barren.

"I'm gonna get the car started. Go fetch your Mom," orders Dad. Good he's ready to go too. I walk up to Mom, still chatting with Karen, and am about to speak when Lindsay approaches.

"Hey, didn't you want me to give Lionel a bath?" she asks.

"Yeah haven't you done that yet?" says Karen.

"No, you never sent him up," answers Lindsay.

"Well then where is he?"

"Don't ask me. Last I checked he was with you."

I realize what has happened before they do. I remember the relief I felt when *he* disappeared. I must not have been his target after all. He has taken Lionel.

12: The Discussion

"So he's been missing for less than an hour?" asks Deputy Yew.

"Yes," answers Mom. Karen Willow is frantically searching the surrounding forest for her son, and Jamie is sitting against his house, head in his folded hands. He probably feels like it's his fault, because I sent him over to look for a possible kidnapper that he didn't find, and now his son is missing. It's not his fault though. He walked right through the fiend without sensing him, so there is no way he could have fought him off. All we possibly could have done better was keep an eye on Lionel at all times, like we should have done. Of course that's probably what *he* was waiting for; an opportunity to strike when no one was looking.

Here I was afraid he was here to take me, but he had his eyes on Lionel.

"Alyssa, can you give me a description of the man you saw?" asks Deputy Yew. Oh right, everyone else thinks a *man* might have taken Lionel.

"Yeah, I mean I didn't get a good look, and I tried to take pictures but they didn't come out, but he was... tall, skinny, and all in black. I didn't see his face at all," I say honestly, although tall; skinny; and black are all abstract words in this case.

"So it didn't look like Jason Larch or Mario Douglas?" he asks. I shake my head. This static entity is probably why Mario and Jason are missing. Yew nods his head to me and begins speaking on his radio. I catch a forlorn, almost apologetic gaze from Jamie and return it.

"It's not his fault," I repeat to myself. If anyone is at fault, it's me. I should have kept an eye all on all three children knowing that thing was near, but I didn't because I was worried about myself. I moan inwardly-I wasn't even keeping a close watch on Adam! At least he is okay, and if I ever see that fiend again, I'm handcuffing Adam to me.

"I just spoke with the sheriff. There aren't very many places he could have gone in such a short time period, so we are going to initiate a search. In the meantime, we need the Willows to give us a list of everyone who came to the party, that way we will have a good number of people to talk to. Maybe one of them got a better look at this guy. Alyssa, do you think you could give an accurate description to a sketch artist?" asks Deputy Yew, hints of stress coming from him.

"No I, I really didn't see his face. I'm sorry," I answer.

"Right, okay listen," he says, turning to my Dad. "You need to take your kids and lock them up at home with an adult present at all times. We've had more than one child disappearing in the same day, so it's best you get your kids to safety," he explains.

"You got it," Dad says, and motions for us to follow him. I can see Lindsay standing in the doorway. She isn't crying, but there's a solemn frown on her face that shows that she is definitely worried about her brother, just like I'd be if Adam had been the one to disappear.

"Eight kids. This man's taken eight kids. When we find him he needs to be hanged," says Mom from behind.

"Nine ma'am. If we don't find the Willow boy, he'll be the ninth," corrects Yew. I bow my head, putting my arm around Adam as we walk toward the car. *Nine kids-ten people missing, this is absurd!* We get into the car and I give one last sympathetic look back to the distraught Willow family. Lionel was kidnapped on his birthday. The whole reason the Willows went through with this party is because they thought it would be a morale booster, but then the perp- the entity strikes. Is it a coincidence that he took Lionel today of all days or did he take him today on purpose just to add to everyone's suffering?

The drive home is silent, and I spend the whole ride looking out the windows to make sure that we aren't still being watched. When we get home, Bubbe greets us at the door.

"I've got supper in the oven, do you want-" she starts, but then she stops when she sees our faces. =

"Oh Lord, what happened?" she asked, but one look from me and she knows exactly what happened. I can convey messages to Bubbe almost as well as I could- can for Shana. I won't give up hope that she's still alive.

She motions us inside. As I enter, the aroma of fresh cornbread hits me. I am normally amazed by how well Bubbe's cornbread turns out, but the bread reminds me of cake, and the cake reminds me of the disastrous party we just came from, and that causes my appetite to plummet. I head upstairs, unsure about what to do. I can get into my pajamas. I've already bathed and I really don't want to bore myself with homework. I don't think I have the focus for it anyway. Maybe I will do some web surfing.

The Slender Man

The internet! Why didn't I think of it before? I can look up the things I've been seeing and experiencing and see if it's some phenomenon that has been dealt with before. I run upstairs with a new motivation guiding my step. I go to my room and flip open my lap top. I have many objects that are pretty old in my collection, but this laptop takes the cake. It's seven years old, and in this day and age, seven years means a lot for technology. We bought it refurbished from a pawn shop, but it's running the latest version of Windows, and has upgraded sound and video cards to boot. The only things it's still lacking in are RAM and storage. It's only got a twenty gigabyte hard drive and half a gigabyte of RAM, so it's not good for anything but storing music and surfing the web.

The hibernation screen takes forever to load into the login screen, and when it does I just press enter. That causes another slow loading screen to play out, and it feels like minutes before my cluttered background piled with different files of no particular organization, ranging from music to funny pictures shows up.

Despite the clutter, I can spot the little Firefox logo perfectly and click on it. Here comes another dull wait. Once the browser finally shows more than a blank white loading screen, I immediately begin typing into the search bar. I start with

"Shadow static disappearing children," and hit enter. I wait a little bit for it to load before it pulls up many different links. I was hoping for an immediate flashing link that would take me to a site that explained exactly what this thing is and how to stop it, but all that pops up are links to a whole bunch of irrelevant multimedia productions. I do some scrolling before deciding that I will need to be more specific. I try "Dark shadow figure that kidnaps children," I hit enter, but then my screen starts fading. It looks like it's doing that whole 'Not responding' bull but then I realize it's getting hazier as if something is wrong with the screen.

I wait a few seconds and then try clicking. The cursor is moving but not opening anything that I click. Is it a computer virus? It could be, I haven't updated my antivirus in like a month. I hold the power button until the laptop turns off, and then I press the power button again for it to turn back on. I sigh, ready for the even longer loading screen that will now be accompanied by a system check. When the screen pulls up, it still has that haze, and then it gets even worse. Now the whiteness fades into blackness, taking all the pretty colors with it. I shake my laptop. No! Why would it crash now of all times? I slam my fist on the keyboard before getting up. I'll just have to us the downstairs computer.

The Slender Man

I turn around and nearly faint with fright when I see a silhouette outside my window. I scream loudly and fall backward onto my bottom. It's *him*, and he's contorting himself. No wait, maybe it's a tree? No, that's impossible-there are no trees outside my window, and even then my almost opaque curtain wouldn't cast a silhouette. What I just saw was more like a shadow cast from the inside. I crawl backward, still on all fours when my parents rush into the room, Bubbe close behind. Dad looks around and assesses the situation before giving me an aggravated look. *Well dude, would you rather a false alarm or me be kidnapped?* I think to myself.

He looks at me for an explanation. I think of an overused lie.

"There was huge spider. It was like a tarantula except, evil looking," I lie. My Dad purses his lips and exits the room.

"Are you alright?" Mom asks politely, but even she doesn't want to wait for a full answer. I give her a quick little nod before turning to face my knees. The entity is still here. It followed me to my house, and now he wants me. I hear the door close and look up in fright, but it's just Bubbe. She's closed the door with us inside.

"Hey," I muster, not sure what this is about. She makes her way through the mess on my floor and sits on my vanity bench and looks at me with a serious look on her face.

"You don't scream bloody murder for a spider," she says. I shrug a bit, not quite sure what to tell her.

"Don't play dumb with me. There's no need for that. I know what's going on," she says.

"You... do?" I ask. "You're seeing things, aren't you?" she asks. I'm not sure whether or not I should trust that she and I are on the same page.

"You won't think I'm crazy?" I ask. She bows her head at me.

"Just because you aren't blind to what's going on doesn't mean you're crazy," she says.

"So you've... seen him? The static monster thing I mean?" I ask.

"That's... one way of describing him," she says.

"What causes it? What is it?" I ask.

She shakes her head. "He's something I hoped I'd never see again," she answers.

"Again?"

"Back when I was little girl in Poland, during the invasion... you couldn't go an hour without seeing him," she starts. "It's easy to just disappear unnoticed when everyone around you is disappearing anyway, don't you agree?" she continues.

"He took people during the Holocaust?" I ask.

"He took *children*," she corrects.

The Slender Man

"So, didn't people notice? Didn't the Gestapo think they ran away or something and punish the parents?"

"Sweetie, those were the same men that threw kids on the streets while shipping their parents off to camps. Those kids were left to die, and many of the ghettos became feeding grounds for the monster."

"So did he follow you?"

She shakes her head. "When I finally got away from there, I never saw him, at least not until now. Not until the accident."

"So he came and caused the accident?" I ask. That would make sense.

She shakes her head.

"I may be wrong, but I'm pretty sure the accident is what drew him here. If he was here before, children would have been missing a lot sooner."

"Why would the accident draw the fiend here though?"

"I only know what my old Rabbi told us about him when kids began disappearing in my neighborhood. We had taken to gathering together as much as we were allowed, to gain safety in numbers. I don't know much about him, but I know that he thrives on human misery. The Rabbi said that there were Jewish tales of the creature; that it loosely mimicked the form of a man, and always appeared in times of suffering-which you know our people have had our share of. Maybe it was the death of so many children at once, or the despair the survivors felt and the way their families worried about their safety that drew him here."

"What about Mario? He's an adult. Do you think he-"

"I think the fiend has something to do with the driver's disappearance yes. I've never- seen him take an adult, but with the amount of guilt someone like Mario would suffer when he recovered, I think the monster wouldn't have been able to resist. It always claims the physically and emotionally weak, and those who have been worn down by some prolonged strong negative emotion."

I look at the ground. He takes the weakest. Jason was strong, but he was so focused on his anger and making everyone around him pay, that the anger had pretty much become his entire existence. Lionel wasn't involved with the crash, but he only turned five today, and he'd been ill, so he'd be weak as well. Shana was always paranoid, and felt doomed for the worst as soon as she heard about the accident. Leanne was consumed with jealousy and hatred for me just because Adam survived. Plus the others I don't know about. They were all vulnerable in some way. They could be led or taken-

The Slender Man

"So what does he do when he's chosen someone? I've seen something watching us, but so do all the people it has taken. Except from what I know they have seen it in the form of their deceased siblings."

"That's what I mean by weakened. If it can get you to come to it by using your own pain against you, it will. Once it's chosen someone, it marks them for its own. I don't understand how, but according to what the Rabbi said and what I observed many times in Poland, and what is now happening here, I think he somehow attaches himself to those he wants and functions as a parasite. Those he's marked to take become ill, they begin to weaken physically and... they always have nose bleeds. He uses their fear to keep them from sleeping and wear them down more, keeping a constant stream of negative emotion. That's why he appears to certain people."

I think about that. The static and vibration in my bones I feel when he's near...maybe that's his energy interfering with mine-like the way some types of electronics interfere with a television or radio and cause static. I wonder if once he has locked onto you as his next target, the static becomes constant. The thought of that fills me with an even bigger sense of dread.

"But he's everywhere. He was just outside my window. He's in my dreams, He's-

"The Rabbi said he's not from this world, but from... ha'olam tsil, a shadow world, and that his interaction with our world is limited. To think of it in modern terms that you can understand, imagine its world as being another dimension, parallel to ours. Pockets of human misery creates thin areas in the veil between the two dimensions, allowing him to leak through... just as a shadow at first, insubstantial. It's very difficult for him to pass through in corporeal form.

"As he appears in his shadow form and generates fear, getting people to focus their thoughts on him, his connection with this world becomes stronger, and he's able to draw people through the veil into the shadow world. Once he's drawn a child through, he establishes a solid physical totem somewhere that allows him easy passage from his own world to his newfound hunting ground. The totem is a physical representation of him. The more children he takes, the stronger his foothold in that area. I don't know if the totem is always the same, but in Poland, that totem was a tall, strange tree that appeared overnight."

"The tree!" I shout. Bubbe looks at me quizzically. "There's a dark tree in the middle of the woods on that route I jog. I never saw it until people started going missing. Would that be it?" I ask.

Bubbe leans back. "How far away is it?"

"It's almost two miles into the woods," I say. "And Shana said that Denise needed her help in the woods, and Adam, when we found him the other day it's like he was heading right for it. It's-"

A look of horror appears on her face.

"I can't have this. Not this close to my grandchildren," she says to herself.

"Well, how do we fight him?" I ask.

She shakes her head.

"You don't. You run from him."

"Won't he follow us?"

"I think he won't stray too far from his tree till he's ready to set up another one. That's why none of the kids from the neighboring cities are gone, but if he's got this many children, and he's this close to us...You children need to stay with your aunt and uncle." Our Aunt Kendra and Uncle Dan live in Michigan though.

"I'm gonna go speak with your parents," she says, getting up.

"Bubbe wait!" She stops.

"How come you can see him, and Jamie Willow walked right through him without noticing?" I ask.

"He appears to people who've suffered, and those who are suffering," she says quietly.

She reaches into the neck of her white floral blouse and pulls out a necklace. She unclasps it from behind her neck and hands it to me. I take it in my hand and my jaw drops open. She just handed me her Star of David necklace that must be as old as my Mom. Its outer coating has long degraded into nothing but copper, and it has the weight of a half dollar.

"I know you don't have much faith in talismans, but it would make me feel a whole lot better if you wore this. You can call it my good luck charm," she says.

I'm almost in tears. I've never seen her without this. She'd chop off her left hand in order to keep this, and now she's handing it over to me? I look back up and hug her tightly. After the hug she gets up and leaves the room to go express the urgency of having Adam and me flee the state. I put the necklace on and feel its weight drop down as I slide it into my shirt. I wait in my room, pondering the situation.

We're dealing with some sort of static shadow monster that thrives on pain, and takes children through to his world. What does it do to the children though? Does it kill or torture the ones it takes? Is it torturing poor Shana and Lionel right now? I can't ignore the possibility. Is it really as old as Bubbe says it is, or are there many of them, a whole race even? That thought terrifies me. I suddenly feel that I don't want to be alone and head downstairs.

I hear Bubbe discussing the little vacation with my parents. She's imploring them to take us to

The Slender Man

Asheville and get us on the next flight first thing in the morning before some "sick child molester" hurts her babies. Her persuasion skills even force me to smile. I'm not excited about going to see my aunt and uncle. They're very dull people, but if it means safety for both Adam and me, who can argue? I see that dinner has already been served. It's cornbread, beans, and steak. I sit at the table and am intimidated by the huge amount of food Mom absentmindedly lumped onto my plate. She's preoccupied with her argument with Bubbe.

"Dan and my sister both work full time, there's no way I can expect them to take a sudden afternoon off to pick up my children on a hunch."

"Then you have them wait outside their house until they get off work. God knows it's worth waiting for a few hours if it means they won't get snatched in broad daylight."

I force as much of the food down as quickly as possible, but only end up finishing about half of it. I don't like wasting food, but I don't like vomiting either, so I casually get up and just scrape the food in the trash. Mom is on the phone with Aunt Kendra now.

"Yes, alright that's great, thank you," Mom says half-enthusiastically.

"What's the verdict?" I ask.

"Any time after six; pack your bags," she says.

169

I go upstairs, but don't immediately pack my bags. I get changed into some pajamas, chancing quick glances around the room to make sure the monster isn't ready to creep up on me, and then I go to grab a suitcase out of my closet. It's not very visible in the jumbled mess of my closet, but it pulls free with a quick yank of the handle. It's a small purple and black zebra stripe suitcase from Wal-Mart. I used to think it was the coolest thing, until I realize just how easy it is to stick the zippers.

I decide I'll help clean up my room a bit by choosing from the various clothes I have scattered about- at least the ones that don't appear dirty. After finding enough shirts and pants to almost fill the suitcase, I determine that the remaining clothes in the floor must all be dirty and kick them into one big pile. I go into my drawers and retrieve socks, underwear, and a few extra items such as a belt and some hair clips just to be sure. I throw some toiletries in, and set my purse on top. Mom would kill me if I leave my schoolbooks so I take my school backpack and set it beside the suitcase. I don't feel like going through it to make sure there are no hidden knives or- oh right, my Mace. I reluctantly remove the canister from my keychain and set it on my vanity. I won't be able to bring that.

The Slender Man

After I think I have everything. I seal up the suitcase, set the backpack on top and take a deep breath.

"I'm ready for bed," I say aloud. The eventful day has made me sleepy, though truthfully it's probably the sickness combined with the exercise. It's only now that I realize that I have to reopen the suitcase to get my toothbrush.

After I retrieve my toothbrush, I head to the bathroom and hear Bubbe in Adam's room. She must be packing his suitcase too. After a good rinse of the face and brushing my teeth, I set the toothbrush on top of the suitcase instead of back in. After all, I'll need it in the morning won't I? I shut the light off and hop in bed.

Great, now I get to be left alone with my thoughts. My memories are no longer a safe place to retreat, and as worries of Shana, Lionel, and concerns for my own safety set in, my drift into sleep isn't so peaceful either. In fact, I hear that static howling now. I try and frown, but it's not happening.

I open my eyes, and this time there's no mistake. He's come for me this time. He's right here in front of me. He's standing upright, and with me lying down I can't even see his face. I feel tears of fear, anger, and frustration surging. Why can't I just be left alone?

I feel the static embrace ready to constrict me again. I will not just give in and go quietly into the shadow world. I begin pushing out with my arms and rocking back with my legs. I'm not going to panic this time. No, now that he's here I'm going to beat him at his own game. I open my mouth and try to let out all the vocals I can. I can hear myself exhale over the already present static wind, but still no moan. *Keep trying,* I tell myself.

The fiend looms over me. His shape is constantly shifting, still unable to maintain perfect motionlessness, and yet he's still able to convey that impression of something perfectly still, watching you. I feel his invisible grip tighten, and terror sets in, making my teeth itch. I want to close my eyes. I want to blink! But I fear if I do he will only get stronger. Shana's words echo in my head. *He wants me to sleep. He wants me to go to sleep.* I feel fluid trickling down my nose. I can tell it's blood by the coppery tang that is sliding down the back of my throat. I feel myself getting weaker under his influence. *It's going take me! I'm going to be the tenth.*

I'm trying to scream at the top of my lungs now, hoping that someone in my house will come and wake me, but all I can do is let out a heavy breath. I need help. *Won't Bubbe have stayed awake to patrol us in our sleep?* I'm hyperventilating. I can't let him take me. I feel him back up. *Is he retreating?* No, he bends down so I can see his face... or I can see where his face would be, if he was an actual man.

He has no face. It's all blackness, and I can only look for a second before my eyes burn. I guess it is not possible for the human eye and brain to process the visual input of this being from another dimension It's just so...wrong...that trying to look directly at it results in a disconcerting vision like a combined effect of a strobe light flashing on static. I instinctively close my eyes to dull the stinging pain, but immediately realize my mistake. Now I can't open my eyes anymore. Its static grip grows stronger and now it's becoming painful. I can sense his face get even closer to me and the closer his head gets to mine, the louder the static ringing gets. I feel my head vibrating as if hearing something this unnatural is going to burst my eardrums. It's resonating throughout my mind, as if it's trying to say something to me. I can make out syllables. It's saying something. It's saying, "Alyssa!"

13: The Nightmare

"Alyssa! Alyssa, wake up! I need your help," I hear. I open my eyes. I can still feel the static immobilizing me, but it's receding. I look and see the monster still looming above me, but I recognize that voice. "Alyssa!" I hear again and the monster leans in, this time touching me with hands, Shana's hands. *Shana*!

I jump up, but immediately stumble forward and fall forward off the bed at Shana's feet. My body is numb. I can still hear the howling wind. I try to move, and can see my body responding, but I can't feel what I'm doing. I can't gauge the amount of strength I'm putting into pushing myself off the floor, and I certainly can't feel enough to balance. I stumble over again. Shana bends down and puts a hand on my arm. I feel a jolt. It's not exactly electricity, but the shock courses through my veins and I can feel a bit of control return. It's only a bit, but it's enough for me to let Shana help lift me up.

I rise to my feet and look at her. She looks... dark and scared. I feel the impulse to lean forward and hug her, but I know something is wrong. I look around and see how dark the place has gotten, yet I can see. "Am I dreaming?" I ask Shana. Shana shakes her head.

"I don't know, but he's had me here for a while," she answers. I take a few steps, trying to get used to the lack of coordination this... dimension, gives me. "I need your help Lyss. I can't stay here," she says. As I move around I notice a field of illumination follows, as if I'm holding a flashlight or something. I look around for the source of light, but everything more than ten feet away from me is immersed in almost total blackness. I look at myself and realize that the light is emanating from me! I am still in the pajamas I was wearing, but my body is distorted and shifting, like, like *him*. It's almost like I'm not solid. I look at Shana and notice that her body is doing the exact same thing, except she is dark. Most of her form is utter blackness.

"Where are we?" I ask. Shana bows her head and moves toward the door. She opens it, and I can see part of the hallway, but everything else is dark. With great effort, I walk through the doorway and look around at my house. It looks almost the same as it usually does, but it has the same eerily dark quality, kind of like it's lit with a black light, but without the illumination. And, it feels empty. I feel a surge of fear as I realize that the monster must have sucked me into his realm-into the shadow world Bubbe told me about. What if I've just disappeared from my bed?

"Alyssa!" Shana cries.

"I need you to help me. I need to get out of here," she continues. I feel the longing I've had to see her well up. Has Shana been watching me from here the whole time? I have to use the wall for balance as I move through the hall. I have to check on Adam, but as I push on his door, I think. *What do I want to see*? Do I want to see Adam lying in bed or not? If he's here that could mean the fiend has sucked him in as well, but if he's not then it could mean the same thing. I push his door, but it won't open. As I push I feel surges of static pushing back against me, through my already numb body. I can't get through.

"Alyssa, come here," Shana pleads.

"I can't! I need to get in here!" I shout with frustration.

"It won't work," she says. I look back at her long enough to see her face distort a bit and wince in response. Shana waits at the top of the stairs and I move over to her, not quite ready to descend. Why can't I get into Adam's room? I turn and look back at it when I feel a wave of the howling static hit me. I can hardly keep my eyes open as I tumble down the stairs. I feel like I'm probably injured, but the pain is dulled by the strange numbness. I can't say that's good, because it's hard to tell if my injuries are serious.

I'm a little dizzy from the fall, but as my vision returns I see the shadowy Shana atop the stairs. She's not even rushing to help me. I close my eyes, taking a breath before I pull myself up on my own. I open my eyes and am shocked to see Shana already at the bottom of the stairs. She's standing over me with the same posture she was at the top of the stairs. It's the same stance she's had since she woke me up. Something tells me she didn't just jump down the steps, and I didn't hear any footsteps.

She bends over and helps me stand up, but before I'm even in a full standing position to make sure I'm still okay to walk, I feel her push me toward the door. The front door? Where does she want me to go? The door is ajar and I pull it open. I'm surprised that when I open the door I can see more than ten feet ahead of me. I can see the shapes of houses, mailboxes, hedges and everything in my neighborhood. There's no moon or apparent source of light, but I can see them. It's such a weird sensation to see without light that it only adds to the confusion I'm already feeling.

Shana pushes me again, but when I turn angrily to look at her she's already in front of me. It's like she tackled me in a rush to get ten feet in front of me, but that doesn't make any sense. I want to help her, I really do, but it doesn't seem like she's as scared or upset as I would be if I'd been stuck in a place like this. I know she's been here for days, so maybe she's gotten used to it, but still I can't see her behaving this way the first opportunity she has to get my help. I follow her down the street, but as I do, I look around. I notice some of the areas, particularly other streets, don't illuminate as I pass by. It's as if I'm not supposed to venture down there, like my path has already been predetermined.

I get the eerie feeling that something is watching me, and I'm starting to be afraid of the way Shana is leading me. She doesn't appear scared at all. She doesn't seem like she's desperately trying to attain my help, and even if she really is, what does she want me to do? I stop walking. What *does* she want me to do? It's only now that I actually stop and think about it. I'm a fifteen year old unarmed girl who is barely capable of walking normally. All I can do is run. I remember Jason and Shana- at least normal Shana in the normal world. Both of them claimed that their siblings appeared to them pleading for their help and then both of them disappeared.

Shana was even afraid to fall to sleep. She must have realized that it wasn't Denise speaking to her. Does that mean that this figure in front of me isn't Shana?

"Alyssa, we have to hurry," she beckons impatiently. I shake my head. No, this isn't Shana. It's *him*. I turn and run, or at least try to run. It's nearly impossible to get a good stride going in this environment. I hear a scream. It's a loud bloodcurdling shriek coming from Shana.

I turn and look at her and see the *he* is upon her. He's not just beside her though. He *has* her. Terror consumes me and I am frozen in place, unsure how to act. So, was I wrong? Can I still separate Shana from this thing's grasp? I try and run to where they are, but with each step closer, the more my eyes hurt. It hurts to look at him, but maybe if I can just pull Shana away from him... He didn't come near when I was with her until now. Maybe that's it then. Shana finally found a way to sneak away from it and then came to get me. Maybe I- or the light around me is some kind of home base where he can't get to her, or maybe he can only get to people if they're alone, and by running away I've just condemned her.

Every step closer I get the howling static gets louder and more intense, and by the time I'm within about ten feet of them I can hardly hear her cries over his static. I get closer and open my eyes just in time to see him disappear. Shana is standing there, hugging herself. She appears shaken. Relief surges through me, and this time I hug her impulsively.

"I'm sorry. I didn't know that he would come."

"Where were you going?" she asks.

"I don't know. I thought you were-"

"I need you to help me," she repeats. She sounds like a broken record, but she's communicating more than she was able to right before she disappeared, so maybe she is recovering. I'm surprised she has recovered even this small amount of her personality in this realm. She forces me off of her. Apparently hug time is over, and the sudden loss of her support causes me to nearly fall over. She resumes walking and I follow.

"Shana. Shana you need to talk to me. I don't know how I can help you. I don't know what to do," I say.

"You have to follow me," she says without so much as turning her gaze toward me.

"Where are we going?" I ask. She stops and looks at me, her body still distorting in places. She points, and I follow her finger up to the ever so familiar entrance to the forest.

"Into the forest?" I ask. She nods and keeps walking. This doesn't feel right. Shana would give me more information- that is, if she could. Her screaming drew me back, but now that I'm following her again I recall the reason I tried to run in the first place. This may not be the fiend per se, but this just doesn't seem like Shana. Maybe he has some sort of mind control over her.

Whatever it is, I can't just go into the woods, because if Bubbe is right, then that tree is the monster's physical totem and entrance to our world, and the closer I get to it, the less likely it will be that I get back. When we get to the edge of the woods I stop again. I can already tell something is awry. The forest has the same black-light pall cast over it, and just being this close to it makes my body vibrate with fright. It feels like a different, darker place. If what I am in now is some nightmarish dream-world, then whatever is in the forest must be the full-fledged shadow world.

My heart begins racing and I feel the howling static swell into an angry crescendo. Shana turns to me and gestures for me to come on.

"I can't. If I do I won't be able to help you," I reason. Shana's mouth begins wobbling, and I can almost see what looks like a tear falling down her face, but the distortion makes it nearly impossible to discern.

"Please Alyssa, we don't have to go far-"

"...just close enough to him," I finish for her.

"I can't do it. I won't. There's got to be some other way, I can come when we're in the real world and I," but I stop. Would I come if I wasn't in some nightmarish realm? I see the darkness from the woods creeping closer and then the black static figure emerges. Shana looks at me with sorrow as he rises up behind her. He looms over her, coming on like a giant black wave. As it approaches my eyes burn and I avert my gaze, but I look up just in time to see her hand lash out and forcibly grab my arm. She pulls hard, and with my already low level of control over my own body I come forward easily. I do my best to resist, but she seems stronger than she normally is. She has merged with the shadowy darkness from the woods, as if it is sucking her in, and as it absorbs her, I get pulled closer into it. *He's attacking*! I look Shana in the eye and I see her look of sadness distort into a glare. She pulls me closer, and now I'm terror stricken. This is not *my* Shana.

I'm almost past the tree line, which I am convinced that in this dream-world is the point of no return. If I allow myself to be pulled into the forest, he will have me. Her face distorts again and this time it's as if she has no face, just a head. Her features are gone. I feel blood pouring from my nose in a steady flow. Her grip is weakening me! I dig my feet into the ground and pull back. She distorts one more time, and I can clearly see her for the first time, as terror stricken as I am. She's disappearing into the darkness, but she's mouthing something. It's inaudible, but just as she releases her grip from my arm, I catch it. She's saying, "...now! You have to wake up, run!" and then she disappears into the woods.

I see a spectral hand form, identical to the one that touched me in my sleep the night Shana disappeared. I'm ten feet away from it before it grabs me. I take off. I have no idea where to run, but I don't stop to think. I just move. I can't tell if he's following me, but if he is then he has the advantage as long as we're in this realm. I keep stumbling, tripping, and falling. Sometimes I catch myself, and sometimes I fall flat on my face, but I keep getting back up and running. I pass my house and enter the section of the neighborhood that isn't illuminated for me.

I can hear Shana's scream again, and I close my eyes to keep tears from flying out. I'm losing Shana again. There's no way this is some illusion. He has her. He's making her scream as a punishment. I pass another house and turn onto the next street, and then suddenly the environment begins blacking out. It's not the dark shadowy blackness of the monster though. It's freedom, its escape, it's a fence. I collide with the fence, but being so experienced in falls and collisions lately I catch myself before I fall all the way.

I am about to resume my flight when I notice something. I see the moon. It's illuminating the street, and I hear crickets. Their chirping wasn't present five seconds ago. This means that I escaped. I'm awake, and I'm free, but I'm on the same street I fled to in the dream world. On top of that, the numb feeling slowly fades from my body, leaving me full of a feeling of pins and needles so intense that it is painful. Due to all the falls in the other world, I ache with pain in so many places. Whatever just happened, it was no dream.

14: The Branch

I rush back to my house with the pain pulsing with every step. My palms, elbows, knees, and face have all taken blows from my multiple collisions. I can imagine I'm pretty bruised up too. I reach my house and see that the door is wide open like I left it. So the dream must have been some nightmarish trance then. If that's true, then why did no one wake up when I fell down the stairs? It must have been loud. I don't know the exact time, but the sky is a purplish hue of impending sunrise, so it must be sometime after four at the earliest.

I climb upstairs and peek into Adam's room to see that he is still lying in bed, breathing. I can hear

Shana's screams echoing in my mind. It may not have been the real Shana, but there's definitely still some of her in there. She must have fought to tell me to run. Maybe he's using her like a marionette, or impersonating her. Either way, her screams were terrifying, and every time it plays through in my mind my body feels heavier, like I'm ready to collapse. You can imagine how someone would scream if they were being axe-murdered by a psychopath, but this scream is worse. When someone is about to be murdered, they're afraid that they're going to die painfully, but this scream was filled with the knowledge that the escape of death isn't coming.

I don't want to leave Shana like that, but what can I do? I go into the bathroom and rinse the blood and sweat from my face. As I do this I repeat the question in my mind. What can I do? I've always wanted to help Shana, and I was almost positive that the shadow monster is what has her, and now it's been confirmed. Now that I hear- now that I am aware of her fear and pain, I don't know what I can do, but I do know that I can't just leave her. There's got to be something I can at least try. It's the tree he wants me to go to, but if I go to the tree in this state, in the real world, will he be able to hurt me? Maybe if I burn the tree? Dad keeps a spare can of gas in the garage, and I'm sure there are matches around here somewhere for the Shabbat candles. No, I can't do that. That would cause a forest fire that I probably wouldn't be able to escape, and even if I do, I'll be jailed for arson.

What would happen if I cut the tree down though? If that's the fiend's totem, his portal, then if it's destroyed he should go away, or at least slow him down right? Or maybe a new one will pop up in its place. How would I cut it down? I can use a chainsaw, but we don't have one. In fact I don't think there's anything at my disposal I can use to cut down the tree. I can at least bother to check though. I can go out back into the shed. Chances are there's something of use there.

I stop in my room and change first. If I'm going to be out in the cold night air I will need a jacket, and some shoes. I put my hoodie over my pajama shirt and throw on some athletic pants over my shorts. I put on some socks and running shoes and then creep downstairs. I hear a stirring coming from my parents' room and freeze. I'll be damned if my parents don't wake up when I fall down the stairs, but do when I creep down them. After I hear the sound of running water coming from the master bathroom I quickly but quietly escape the house and shut the front door behind me.

As soon as I'm outside, I look around to make sure the monster hasn't returned. After doing so, I run around the side of the house and to the back. In our backyard is a shed, but it's never locked. I don't even think there's much in here. Come to think of it, I don't recall ever being in there at all. I open the shed and wince as it creaks loudly the whole way. I want to sneak in and shut the door but it's so dark in here, and with no windows I'll need the moonlight to show me the way. I wish I'd thought to grab a flashlight, but that would involve scouring the whole house for one and probably waking everyone up. Inside the shed sits a big lawnmower. It's dirty and covered with dead grass. Next to the lawnmower are items useless to me like rakes, a tire iron- a toolbox.

There must be something in there right? I go over to the toolbox and am surprised at how heavy it is. It's big and rectangular, and it takes me a few tries to get the clasps open. After I finally open it a bunch of lazily piled tools fall out and clang loudly. I put my hands to my ears reflexively although it's not what *I* hear that what matters.

After a long pause to make sure my parents aren't rushing out to catch me I sort through the tools and find nothing but wrenches, and wrench-like thingies that I don't even know the name for. None of them so much as have a blade. After a huff and a puff I take one last look around the shed and then leave. I might not be able to cut down the tree after all.

Standing outside the shed I look around with disappointment before something catches my eye.

The Slender Man

You can see the neighbor's yards all the way down the street as the fences are chain-link, but a few houses down I see a pile of chopped wood. They aren't in plastic packages or with anything to hint that they were bought, so that must imply that the people- I'm not sure who they are, we aren't very social with our neighbors- chopped it themselves. I am about ready to hop the fence into the adjacent yard but then I catch sight of their doghouse. It's not particularly big, but I know I've heard dogs barking here before, and they aren't Chihuahuas.

I go around the front way, hoping no one in this neighborhood has a five A.M. appointment. When I reach the house with the woodpile, I sneak around back and am relieved to see no doghouse next to their wood pile. I'm not a thief, but for the sake of trying to save a life- or prevent further kidnappings- I'm sure they wouldn't mind if I borrow-without-asking one of their tools. I try and hop the fence with my normal dexterity, but my bruises flash with pain and I stumble at the top, cutting my thigh on the top of the fence. It's not deep, but it stings and will probably bleed. I don't want to delay though, so I limp over to their shed with one hand on my thigh.

When I reach the doors, I see that they are padlocked, great. I sigh and am about to give up when I see just what I need. There is a large woodcutting axe lazily propped against the pile of wood. I almost laugh when I remember I'm trying to be discreet. I snatch the axe, toss it over the fence and- carefully this time- hop back over. I stick as much of the axe as I can into my jacket. The head is fully concealed, but there are a good six inches of the handle sticking out from underneath.

I reach the edge of the sidewalk, my usual stretch point. Well, I was always careful to stretch before running through the woods, so why not stretch before trying to defeat a monster from another dimension? I do stretch as best as I can with the pain and trying to conceal the axe. I feel like I'm finally ready, but when I'm about to battle-charge into the woods, a little voice inside my head reminds me of what I'm about to do. As I think about my mission, I suddenly feel like it's *not* such a good idea. I am about to venture over a mile into the woods alone so early in the morning that it's pretty much night. These woods are the playground for a shadow entity that's been kidnapping people, and I'm going in based on the hunch that if I cut down an eerie tree everyone will be okay.

I take a step back, but then Shana's screams echo in my head. I have to try otherwise I'll spend the rest of my life regretting it and wondering if I could have saved her. She would do the same for me. I look and see the sun rising. At least I'll have light. I jog off into the woods, doing the best I can to keep the axe from falling out or disemboweling me, but once I get about fifty yards in, I lose the urge to run. I can still hardly see, and I get the feeling that I'm not alone.

I begin walking, slowly but steadily. I listen for any sound that differs from the sound of leaves and twigs crunching beneath me. I still have the axe tucked into my jacket, and I contemplate bringing it out so I will be ready to swing if something jumps out at me. Is the monster even corporeal enough to be hurt by an axe?

I climb the first slope. By now, the sun is casting an orange and pink glow. Another twenty minutes must have passed since I first entered the woods. The forest is still unusually dark though. Maybe it's because I haven't been in the woods this early before, but I don't like the idea of not being able to see far ahead of me. I keep feeling like I'm back in the nightmare, and at times I feel like I've taken a wrong turn. I'm used to looking far ahead of me to determine my path to the clearing, not from tree to tree.

I hear leaves rustling in response to a gust of wind. The wind blows past me and I shudder, not because of any kind of chill, but because of the static wave that passes through me. I tremble and let out a tiny squeak in response. He knows I'm here. I keep walking. I can't stop now. I feel like he's behind me, but I don't dare turn around. Another gust hits me and I close my eyes. I don't want to open them for fear of what I might see. I begin taking very deep and controlled breaths to calm myself. I try and make them as quiet as possible because I don't want him to hear how scared I am if he can't already sense it.

I don't hear any footsteps to signal him following me, but every few seconds another wave of static passes through me, reminding me that he's watching me. I look at the ground, guiding myself forward by memory. I don't know where he is, or how close he is, but he's stalking me. Why isn't it attacking me? Maybe he's having fun toying with me. Maybe he's confused as to why I would come here of my own will and is waiting to find out. If that's the case then it's best I keep the axe hidden under my jacket. Or maybe he needs to wear me down before he can strike.

Whatever it is, I can't show any signs of fear or panic. I can't run. I have to ignore him. I have to pretend he's not there. If I run, scream, or stop, he will know I'm scared. It's harder than it sounds, and with every step I take, with every static wave that pulses through me, I find it harder to keep my wits. Panicky thoughts flood my mind. *What have I gotten myself into? Why didn't I call the police department and have them cut the tree down. Or why didn't I have some other adult come out and do it. Why didn't I at least bring an escort?*

I've set myself up here. I've made the fiend's job easier. As these thoughts set in, I find it harder to draw steady breaths. I take one slow deep breath, but force it all out in an uncontrollable burst, accompanied by an audible squeak or moan that I know he hears. It's harder to walk, and it doesn't help that the more the sun rises, the darker the forest seems to get. Why didn't I bring a flashlight? I didn't come as prepared as I should have.

I feel as if my rib cage is about to crack behind my heart's heavy thuds. I reach another incline. *I'm finally here!* It's only a few more yards and then I can hack away, but he's watching me. Will he let me cut the tree down? Can he stop me? Every time he's been able to immobilize me I was in that state between waking and sleeping. I figure I should be pretty safe since I'm wide awake, but then again I doubt Lionel was asleep when the fiend claimed him.

I pause just past the base of the incline. I'm unsure of how I want to proceed. I could draw the axe and run in with a Rebel yell, or maybe I could creep up and take it by surprise. I can still sense him, awaiting my next step. Maybe he's waiting for me to come within arm's reach of the tree to grab me. Another wave of static comes, and this time I can almost hear a breath as it passes through me. It's as if he's right behind me, ushering me forward. As the wave passes through me, I feel a mixture of fluid running down my face: sweat, tears, and now blood from my nose. My body is weakening.

Is he attacking me now? No, I can't let him. I move up the hill as quickly as my willpower pushes me, but it's still slower than the average walking pace. My brain is screaming at me. *No! No! No!* What else can I do though? I can't run, I can't just stay here, and if I can't go forward he wins without a fight. When I reach the top of the hill, I see the tree, barely visible in the dark forest. It's hard to count exactly how many, but there are now more than nine branches on this tree. It looks closer to a dozen give or take. That's only more proof that this tree isn't just a normal tree.

I approach the tree and I'm only a few feet away from it when I hear Shana's cries coming from it. I close my eyes and jerk the axe out of my jacket. I take one more step, and then feel another static wave. This one is more intense though, and now it's accompanied by a loud monotonous screeching sound. It matches the static pulse but it's shrill and loud, and I half expect my ears to burst from the noise. The screeching becomes one nonstop note. I feel my body going numb, like it was in the nightmare and then I realize what's happening. It *is* attacking me! It's trying to stop me! Then that means- I rush forward with the axe and take a swing. I feel it collide against the tree and yank it back. I feel pain.

The static is pulsing, trying to silence me. I strike the tree again, but this time I think the axe hits one of the branches instead of the trunk. *No!* I can't hit random places I have to knock the tree down. I am about to swing again when I feel another pulse and my arms are almost completely numb. Unfeeling, I still manage to swing the axe again, and again, and again. I don't know what I'm swinging at. My eyes are closed and I am swinging at everything. I'm swinging at the monster. I'm swinging at branches. I'm swinging at the tree. I'm growing weaker. I'm falling to my knees. I- I can't feel anything except for numbing static. I can't hear anything except for the continuous shriek. Has he won? I feel myself weakening, and hear the sound of a branch falling to the ground beside me before I succumb.

15: The Rescue

I come to my senses and find that I'm on the ground by the tree. Blood flows back into my head and I feel nauseous, but the static grip on me weakens. I open my eyes, but close them immediately. *He* is right there. Head tingling and eyes closed, I do my best to propel myself back and crawl out of the way. I feel him grab me again, and at his touch a wave of the burning numbness courses through my body. I open my eyes again and see him there. One of his limbs is attached to me, but I close my eyes once more to stop that pain in my eyes. Jolts of pain come from my torso and arms as well. They are quick, but frequent.

I hear a scream coming from my left. I open my eyes and look to see Shana lying on the ground.

The Slender Man

She's writhing as if trying to crawl. Where did she come from? Is this really her, or more of a nightmare? More flashes of pain shoot through me and I look down and notice that they are coming from the distortions in my body. Every time my body moves like static I feel pain, as if that part of my body is being torn off.

I scream as the ripping pains become even more frequent. I see that the black shadowy limb that's touching me doesn't appear to be an arm. It's like a black vortex that's attached to the monster, somehow appearing solid at the same time. Every time it distorts with static, so do I, and then I get hit with a flash of pain. It's like it's sucking the life right out of me. I roll onto my stomach and crawl away, toward Shana. I stop screaming, although I can't tell if that's my willpower, or if I'm just getting weaker.

I reach Shana and put a hand on her, trying to pull her up with me as I try to stand. She doesn't seem to realize what's going on, but with one look at me, recognition lights her face, and she leans forward on me. She isn't necessarily helping me up but with the shift of balance I find it easier to rise. I feel another jolt of pain, and cringe, but the painful flashes are less intense now.

I'm ten feet or so away from the fiend, ten feet away from the tree. I can't tell which one is hurting me. Maybe it's both, or maybe they're the same thing. I limp away with Shana at my side. I feel pain again, and although it's even weaker than before, with it being the only thing I can feel through the numbness I cry out. What's he doing to me? I'm not bleeding, but it feels like I should be.

"Shana," I say weakly. She doesn't answer, but keeps walking forward with me, leaning on my shoulder. I notice she isn't distorting like she was in the nightmare, like I am now. I think I see why though.

I see another appendage lash out and attach to her, and in response her whole body distorts and she lets out a loud scream. I take a look back at the monster and notice that the limbs attached to us seem to be coming from the upper half of the thing, like- like branches. Is that it then? Is that why the tree kept spawning more branches? Does this mean that his tree gains a new branch for each child he kidnaps? If so, then what happens to us when he takes us in? I'm not sure if that's an answer I want to find out.

With Shana's sudden lack of cooperation we both fall forward onto our knees. I have to get her farther away from the tree. I climb to a semi-standing position as quickly as I can and haul Shana with me. She looks like she wants to help, but has lost sense of what she's supposed to be doing.

I look around while pulling her forward. We are still in the forest, but now it's definitely the shadow dimension version of the forest, and the only source of light is... is me. Another tearing pain, and I fall back to my knees, and the light grows dimmer in response. What does this mean? The light coming from me... is that what he's trying to get rid of before it can- I hear a loud screeching sound. It mimics the sound I heard when the fiend first charged. He's here.

I feel- or at least think I feel a sudden rush of adrenaline and I haul both Shana and myself up in one quick pull. I balance her weight with my shoulder and practically drag her away. I don't know which direction I'm heading, only that it's away from the tree. The shrieking gets louder and begins pulsing. It's pulsing with a distinct rhythm, and seems to be coming from multiple directions. The rhythm- I've heard it before, it's... it's laughter. He's laughing at us. He must be sure we can't escape. I only hope he's wrong. His laugh grows louder and echoes from all directions-from very close to very far and in a variety of volumes and pitches.

I begin screaming at him out of both anger and fear. I feel tears rolling down my face.

"What do you want from us!?" I scream, but my voice cracks. I can feel the numbness growing stronger. Each note of laughter sends a pulse in my direction. My heart is racing and I can't think. I can't move. Shana falls to the ground on my side and causes me to stumble again.

I scream as loudly as I can, trying to block out the ominous laughter that torments me. Covering my ears doesn't seem to work, because even though the laughing sounds quiet, I can *feel* it pulsing through my bones. Each vibration sends another shock of terror and all I want is to get out of here. I'm in agony; he's on me again. I feel myself being pulled back toward the tree. *No!* I didn't come here in vain.

I fight him, throwing punches and kicks, squirming and wriggling. I don't feel myself hitting anything, except for a few trees in my path, and I can feel myself being dragged back to the clearing at a sprinter's pace.

"No!" I scream and continue fighting. I find myself on my stomach and manage to wrap my arms around the trunk of one of the trees. Using it for leverage against the pull of the monster, I pull myself forward, away from the fiend as hard and fast as I can, pain coursing through my body, crying. I'm trying to get back to Shana. I came here for her, and I won't just leave her here.

I crawl forward, and every time I progress to another tree I wrap onto it to keep from the sudden backward tugs, but even though I'm so close to Shana that I can see her through the dark, the light grows dimmer with every pull. He doesn't need me to go to the tree. He just needs to put out the light. He only does it faster if I'm closer to it; if I'm weakened, but now it's too late. I can't find the strength or balance to stand, and even though Shana is standing only a yard from me, the blackness will take me before I can get to her.

Wait… she's standing! I feel a hand on mine. Shana's reaching for me and soon I feel her hand on mine. I feel myself being pulled up to my feet, but at the same time I feel like I've reached the end of my strength. I have an overwhelming sense of dizziness. I can't stand on my own, I can't walk, I can hardly think. I can sense the fiend around me, and vertigo consumes me.

Humans aren't meant to feel this way. Humans aren't even meant to be here. I become lost in my thoughts, answering my own questions. *Why am I here?* I came to free Shana. *How did I plan to do that?* I tried to cut down the tree, but what now? I feel my body convulse, and although I can't see it, I know I've vomited. I feel another tug, and hear a voice, but the voice is muffled by the shrieks of static. "I can't…"

"Alyssa…"

"He's calling my name."

"Alyssa… Lyss!" I feel another pull. I realize I've been dragged a few feet since Shana helped me to my feet and I fell over.

"Alyssa… we have to go," says Shana.

"Don't let him claim you. You'll never get out."
I look up and see Shana still pulling me through the
woods. She's not looking at me. Instead her gaze is
a blank stare. I think she's talking to herself as well
as me.

We can't give up. That's what she's trying to
say, but what do we do? I have no strength. My
only incentive to move is the thought of escaping
with Shana? *But how?* The question repeats in my
mind. I escaped last time didn't I? Yeah, I ran. I ran
out of his grasp and he couldn't hold me. If I can put
enough distance between us and the monster, then
we should make it out okay. I have to keep fighting
though. I have to fight through the numbness,
dizziness, pain, and shrieking.

I gather my last bit of strength together and pull
back on Shana's weight, rising to my feet.

"We have to go," she repeats. There's almost
no light, and all I can see is her face, less than an
arm's length away.

"Let's go," I say feebly. Her hand in mine, we
run. I run with my free hand forward, pushing
myself out of the way of trees that appear in my
path. I can only hope I'm moving forward in one
direction, and not in circles, but there are trees,
slopes, and hills every few feet that we have to
dodge. This involves many turns and twists, and
with no light I have no sense of direction, and with

my many stumbles I'm sure I've gotten turned around a few times.

I feel a rushing wave of howling static. It's pushing from behind us.

"He's coming," mutters Shana.

"He's coming!" she shrieks. Another wave hits me. It's the same thing that happened when I was on my way to the tree with the axe. Except now, he's faster. He's not stalking. He's pursuing, and I feel him getting closer. Shana does too. I can tell through her sobs. She's losing hope. I wish I could get a good look at her face, but it's hard enough getting her to keep up with me.

I feel another pulse. This one weakens me and causes my knees to almost buckle, but I keep moving. The wave must have affected her more than it did me because I feel her slipping. She's lagging behind, failing to keep up. I can't tell if she's just too tired to run any faster or losing consciousness, but I think it's the latter. I have to keep her talking. I cut her off from him and then she pulled me away from him when he had me. Now it's a game of keep-away. I can't tell who he's targeting.

He wants both of us, but I think he can only take one of us at a time. He came after me while I was panicking, and now I can only feel him following us. This must mean he's after Shana. She needs a voice to listen to. She needs to remember that it's my hand she's holding and not his.

"Shana, we're gonna be okay. Just keep running!" I say, trying to shout, but I'm already breathless. He reinforces his laughter, as if emphasizing it in response to me, and I feel a static wave that almost forces me forward, but at the same time I feel Shana's grip weaken as if she's being pulled back. She needs to talk to me. I need to know she'll make it.

She screams. I look, but I can't see what has her. I can't see what he's doing. I run into a tree, and am glad that the numbness works to distance the pain. Otherwise I wouldn't be able to stay on my toes.

I wrap around the tree, jerking Shana. I feel a lot of resistance and hope I didn't just dislocate her shoulder or anything. She's fallen to her knees, and is still screaming. It's that same scream she gave me in my original nightmare.

"No, I won't let you take her away from me again. You're not going to hurt her anymore," I say aloud. We're not going to escape him with me dragging her like this. I turn around and pick her up. It's nearly impossible, because I already had a hard to time getting used to running while almost completely numb, but without the numbness I probably wouldn't be able to lift Shana at all.

The Slender Man

I can tell my speed isn't that of a sprinter, it barely would pass for a brisk walk, but I came here for her, and I'm not leaving without her. Her screaming fades into cries and I can tell she's slipping. She's close enough now that I can see her face. It looks like she's dying right in my arms. "Shana!" I scream.

"We're almost there! Shana, hold on! Almost!" but I'm not sure how true that even is.

In the nightmare I only ran a few dozen meters from the tree line where his presence was the strongest, and we haven't even left the woods yet, but we're going in another direction I'm sure. Does he have control over the whole forest, or just a certain distance? I hope that whatever the truth is, I can make it out with Shana.

I push one of the trees with my shoulder to work around it, and then that sense of vertigo hits me. The tree grabs me, but it's not just a tree. It's him, it's his static hand. I scream loudly as he touches me. My body distorts with that meat-grinding pain at the contact point. I bite my tongue, so hard that I taste blood.

"You're not going to take me now…" I have to keep going. I march forward and away at a snail's pace. My body feels like I'm being eaten alive from the inside out but I do my best not to scream. I won't give him power. I won't give up.

His grip won't relent though and I can hear his static screeching all around me again. He's fighting hard now, there's no way I can- *he's fighting this hard*! He must be panicking. That can only mean that I'm very near.

"We're almost there Shana! Stay with me, it's just a little longer," I cheer. I have some feeling return, telling me that I'm almost out of this world. I sprint, all or nothing now. I can only hope I don't run headfirst into tree.

My arms are burning from the pressure of Shana's weight. Suddenly, I feel my balance return and can run more steadily. My legs are burning hot lead, and my feet feel like they're about to shatter. My clothes are covered in sweat, constricting me, slowing me down. It's nearly impossible to get enough oxygen, but as all of these feelings return to me, so does light. *Light!* I can see.

It's a little past dawn now and the sun has risen. I can see the edge of the woods, only a few yards away. I move with unrelenting speed. I can still sense him here. He's going to try and pull Shana and me back. I remember the sudden anxiety I had of being pulled back into the woods the first time I ran from the tree. That seems more likely to happen this time, but I'm not about to let it. It's only twenty paces away...nineteen... fifteen... ten. I'm holding my breath, but I'm almost there.

The Slender Man

"We're almost there Shana! We're there! We're free!" I can't say it above a whisper though. I don't have the breath. We emerge onto a road and I hear a honk and turn to see a police car. I close my eyes expecting to be hit, but the tires screech with no impact. I look to see Deputy Yew step out and run over to me. I laugh a tired, tortured, but triumphant laughter, and fall to my knees. *Who's laughing now shadow?*

"We made it Shana, the police are here," I say. She doesn't respond.

"Shana?" I look down at her. She isn't moving.

"Shana!" I yell. She's dead.

16: The Shrink

I can't hear anything. I see an ambulance has pulled up with its siren's blaring. I see men shouting at me, trying to pull Shana from my arms, and I see Deputy Yew. He's also talking to me, but I can't tell if he's helping the paramedics or trying to comfort me. It's hard to tell from the expression on his face. Most notably of all, I can't hear my own screams. I don't want to let go of Shana. I've made it this far, how could I fail? She was alive only moments ago, and now that we've escaped she's not even breathing. How could I make it when she couldn't? I put all the work into getting in and getting out, I was almost beaten, and yet I escaped-and I thought I'd freed Shana.

The Slender Man

Even still, the monster made sure that there was no truly happy ending. I won't be escaping to Michigan with peace of mind knowing the people I care about are safe. I was so close...

Shana is wrenched from my desperate grip and I fall forward. I don't have the strength or willpower to hold myself up, and yet I don't hit the ground. Deputy Yew has his arms around me and is pulling me to my feet. He's still saying something to me, and even though I've stopped screaming, I still can't hear him.

I watch as the paramedics try to resuscitate Shana. She's not bleeding and there are no wounds on her, so they believe there may be hope for her, but I know there isn't. I know that whatever the monster did to her won't be undone by CPR. Deputy Yew puts me in the back of the police car. I can't tell if I'm being arrested or just given a ride. I'm not in handcuffs and I haven't done anything illegal-well, aside from minor theft of the axe, and if the police know about it I'm sure arresting me isn't a priority.

Throughout the car ride, I lay lengthwise across the whole backseat, crying. My hearing slowly returns but everything is still distorted. I can hear Yew saying something on his radio, and I can hear my own sobbing. Shana... I failed her. The car stops and seconds later the door opens. I'm not immediately yanked out, but I guess they figure out that I won't be moving on my own, and some police officers remove me from the car.

We are at the sheriff's station. It's a short brick building with a small cement flight of stairs leading up to a set of dark brown wooden double-doors. I've never actually been inside before now. Yew and one of the other officers guides me in and has me sit on a plastic chair near reception. I look around. There's a lot of running around going on. I can't tell if this is how they've been working since the cases of the other children, or if they are doing this in response to finding me with Shana. I can hear everything that's going on, and eventually I hear footsteps approaching me.

"Lyss," says Mom. She puts her arms around me, but I don't hug her back. I can't. I feel like I'm frozen in place by grief. If I wasn't surrounded by people, I'd be a perfect victim for that fiend, no strength physically or mentally.

"As soon as we found you missing we notified the police. We feared the worst! What the hell were you doing?" she asks. Maybe the police haven't told her about Shana yet.

"Ma'am," speaks Sheriff Fraser, emerging from the sheriff's office. "We need to talk. Will you step into this office for a moment?" he asks.

"I'm not leaving my daughter," says Mom. "Alyssa, answer me."

The Slender Man

Dad walks from around the corner and puts a hand on my shoulder. I immediately think he's going to come off as angry and try to scold me, but he has a look of relief on his face. Bubbe and Adam are here too. Bubbe has her poker face on. She knows what was involved with this and isn't going to waste time scolding me or announcing her relief just yet. Adam looks blank. He must have just been wakened and with him still being sick, he probably doesn't fully comprehend what's happening. I lock eyes with Bubbe for a moment, but then I see figures emerge from behind her.

Here comes Deputy Yew and another person. I haven't seen the man behind him before. He looks like he was just awakened too, but is fully dressed in a grey business suit and shaven. The expression on his face shows me a man that hasn't had his coffee yet. Both of the men step into the sheriff's office behind where the sheriff is standing. "Well, it's very important in regards to your daughter," continues the sheriff.

"Then talk to us right here," snaps Dad.

The sheriff pauses as if to ponder the situation for a moment, and then finally spurts out. "Alyssa was found with the Hawthorn girl. One of my deputies found her carrying her corpse from the forest," he says.

My mind blanks for a moment at his words. His recap brings the memory back up, masking all

211

sound in the area. I close my eyes as more tears pour out. I remember trying to look at her face while carrying her. I told her we'd make it, that we were almost there, but I couldn't see her face. Was she dead then or dying? If I'd just run faster. If I was just a minute faster my friend would be alive. I hear static, and open my eyes.

"No... I don't want you. Go away," I mutter aloud. I know he can hear me. I open my eyes and look for it, but all I see are looks of worry and bewilderment from my family and the officers within earshot.

"You think she was involved with the disappearance? Shana and Alyssa were like-"

"Sisters, I know. Every summer my niece comes to visit and brings her best friend along with her. I know what that bond is like. Those two are inseparable. They'd take a bullet for each other. I think that may be why Alyssa was able to find her. It's the only explanation considering that we've scoured the woods for days with no luck. Alyssa is the person we *least* suspect, but we still need to question her."

"About what? Where she found Shana? She's speaking gibberish for crying out loud she's not going to be able to answer questions like that in her state!" says Dad.

"We know, but we need to get all the information we can, so we need to help your daughter. In this office is a psychiatrist, Doctor Filbert, and with your permission we'd like to have him speak with your daughter. This could help us both," he explains.

A shrink? He wants me to see a shrink? For what? I just watched my best friend die, of course I'm going to be upset, that doesn't mean I'm crazy! I want to shout it, and I even try to, but all of my anger dissolves into further sadness, and all I can do is hold my mouth open for a few seconds. My parents agree to it against my will. I don't need a doctor, but there's little I can do to resist being guided from my seat into a private interrogation room in the back corridor of the building.

As I'm being escorted through the hallway, I see glimpses of him- the static fiend that took Shana from me. Every time he appears I want to scream out of both anger and fear, but each time it's more anger than fear. He wants me to be afraid, and he's even more hell-bent on stalking me now. He's appearing around every corner, every corridor, and every window. He's not in the interrogation room, though.

I always imagined these rooms were supposed to be mostly white, but this room looks just like every other room in the building. It still has the blue carpeting the rest of the station does, and the walls are more of a beige than white. The table is grey and the chairs are blue metal foldout chairs like we have at our school. Dr. Filbert, the bald shrink, sits at one end of the table, coffee in hand. He motions for me to sit opposite him, but even so the officer escorts me to the chair to help me sit. There is a giant mirror on the wall. That must be one of the one-way windows. I'm sure the sheriff and Deputy Yew are watching, but I'm wondering if my family is too.

Just how many people are interested in how I found Shana? It can't be hard for them to piece together even without me. I wandered into the woods and found her. That's far from the truth but still something they can go by.

"Can you tell me your name?" asks Doctor Filbert. I'm surprised by his voice. It doesn't sound aged or deep or anything you'd expect a man of his stature to have. Instead it's soft but high, like someone who's trying to coo a child.

"Maybe I should start," he continues. I want to cringe at that voice; it makes him sound like a pedophile.

"My name is Dean Filbert. I'm a psychiatrist and I'm here to help you," he explains. I look down at the table. I can't watch him when he talks.

"I need you to talk to me. If you want you can tell me what happened in your own words, or I can ask you questions?" he tries. I stare at the table. I feel a wave of static pass through me again. That fiend- he, is watching. I grit my teeth behind my lips.

"Alyssa, how are you feeling?" What kind of question is that? My best friend just died and I'm being haunted by a monster. How does he *think* I'm feeling?

He says a few more things but I just tune him out. What am I going to do? I couldn't get Shana out and now the entity seems to be following me. Will he wait until I'm alone and then strike? Is he strong enough to pull me into his domain now? I imagine he is basking in my pain right now. If only I could push my emotions away like a sociopath. If I could not care, then maybe he won't desire me so much.

I look up and catch a flash of annoyance flit across Doctor Filbert's face, but he wipes it off. I guess it's unprofessional for a psychiatrist to seem angry with one of his clients. There's a knock on the door. "Enter," says Filbert in that peevish voice. I actually do wince this time. I am surprised to see that Bubbe is the one at the door. Sheriff Fraser is behind her.

"Let me talk to her a bit. I might be able to help," she suggests coolly. Doctor Filbert sizes Bubbe up before reluctantly agreeing. He waves her in. "In private. That means just the two of us. No one needs to see or hear our conversation. Am I understood?" Bubbe asks the sheriff. Sheriff Fraser doesn't show any sign of disagreement. He gives her one of those 'whatever works' nods and then escorts a now-openly-very-annoyed looking Doctor Filbert out.

Bubbe sits down across from me. I'm wondering what she's going to say, but she doesn't speak immediately. Maybe she's giving them time to clear the adjacent room out. I wouldn't give them the benefit of the doubt though. Then again Bubbe probably already told my parents, who are making sure there are no eavesdroppers.

"That was a very brave thing you did," Bubbe starts. I look in her in the eye. "I can't say I would have let you do it, but you did the right thing. I want you to know that."

What is she saying? I endangered myself and failed to succeed in my mission.

"You can't keep blaming yourself. I know you did what you could. I've never seen someone succeed in the way that you have," she continues.

"Succeed?" I ask feebly. She nods her head.

"When this thing takes children, they never return. Shana is the only person I've known to come back. You saved her."

I shake my head. "She's dead... she died just before I escaped," I say.

"You're right, she's dead, but is that such a bad thing?" she asks.

The Slender Man

I look at her with bewilderment. What is she talking about? Of course her dying is a bad thing. "Wha- what are you saying?" I ask.

"I don't know the details. I don't know how you did it, but when you went in and found Shana, she was alive. Wasn't she?" she asks. I feel my head throbbing with the painful reminder. I nod my head.

"That means she was alive the whole time she was missing," she continues.

"I imagine it wasn't pleasant... in *his* world. How did it feel?" she asks.

I find her order of questions odd, and not in a good way, but I answer her, sincerely hoping that no one else is watching lest I be pronounced certifiably insane.

"It was dark, and painful... he was laughing at me. I couldn't see or feel anything... except pain and fear," I explain.

"And how long were you in there?" she asks.

"It was around... less than an hour... I don't know. It felt like days," I say.

"Now how long was Shana in there?" she asks.

I pause for a moment. "...days."

"If minutes feel like days to you, how long do you think days felt to her?" she asks. I bow my head. Shana was subject to that- no, he'd absorbed her until I cut her off, so she was subject to worse than I was, and for days at end. Her screams... they were very real.

"I think your friend would thank you if she could. She may not be alive to do it, but you did the next best thing. You saved her from him, and gave her death. If she'd remained trapped in that monster's world, her parents would have been prevented from having closure. Now they can sit shivah for Shana and eventually make peace with her loss instead of being tormented by not knowing for the rest of their lives," she says. I shake my head.

"He still killed her though. He probably still has her spirit in his clutches."

Now she shakes her head. "I don't think so. I think he needs them alive, weakened, yes, but alive. If he tries to take them when they're too weak, then they'll only end up dying, and he'll lose them," she says. I close my eyes. Do her words ring true? Have I really saved Shana from a fate worse than death... by bringing her death?

The thought sounds dark... in fact I think I actually feel worse for a few minutes. That means she was tortured all that time... how I felt... she felt that and much more and for a longer period. I shake the thoughts out, now- hopefully, all that is behind her, and she can rest in peace like Bubbe just said.

"You can't keep ignoring the doctor like this though. You and I may both know you're not crazy, but if you don't prove that to him, he can have you locked up, and then there will be little we can do to protect you from *him*," she says.

"What can protect me at all?" I ask.

"You have to listen to me Alyssa, give these men the information they want. Even if it's just a wild goose chase, it will give them something to go on, and then we'll figure something out," she explains. I admire her wisdom and nod my head.

"I'll see you in a few minutes." She exits the room, and almost immediately after her departure, Doctor Filbert reenters. This time he is holding a bottle of Sprite. He waves the bottle, nonverbally asking if I want it. I could use a soda, at least if I'm going to be dealing with this guy.

He sits back in the chair opposite and doesn't even wait for me to finish opening the Sprite before he starts talking. He doesn't repeat his first questions, instead he moves on. He asks a lot of redundant 'how am I feeling, what am I thinking about right now' questions that make me think he's not really the best doctor to have out here. Eventually he does try to figure out exactly what I was doing.

It's mutually understood between Bubbe and me that I can't just tell him that I ventured into the woods trying to rescue Shana from an entity, but I do have to give him a story that adds up. I'm not able to just think up a lie, not with my current state, but I do manage to leave essential parts out to make a linear story. It seems like his whole inquiry will answer the questions the police may have too.

"So let me get this straight, you were distraught about the loss of your friend. So you proceeded to steal a woodcutting axe to take your anger out on a tree that always bothered you when you ran by it?" he asks.

I nod, hoping that doesn't 'prove' to him that I'm mentally insane.

"While venting on this tree, you cut one of the branches off, but then you hear something. You chase after it and find Shana lying on the ground in the woods. She didn't appear to have been attacked or raped, but looked like she had just run from something and was too exhausted to push further?" he continues.

I nod again. "You try and help her to her feet and while she is leaning against you, you hear a noise and think it might be whoever kidnapped her coming to take her back, so you pick her up and run as fast as you can in a panic?" he asks.

I nod for a third time. "And you managed to get away from him- if he was chasing you in the first place, and that's where the police found you?"

"That's correct," I say.

"Alright, so that answers that. Now you said you were feeling anguished at the loss of your friend, which is what led you to attack the tree. Tell me, have you ever had any sort of destructive thoughts towards another person? For instance, people you don't like, or maybe yourself?"

"You're asking if I want to hurt people because of what happened to Shana?" I ask a little miffed.

"Or yourself," he corrects. I shake my head.

"No, I didn't even have too much of a problem with the tree. I just, don't have a diary or punching bag and it's creepy anyway, it felt like it would help," I explain, hoping he isn't about to say I'm a danger to those around me.

He gives me a little nod before speaking again in his squeaky voice. "Alright, so I can understand how you're feeling. I've met a lot of people who take their emotions out in worse ways, but a lot of their actions start out like this, and then they sink into depression. I am going to suggest you do something to help with your emotions. You should maybe invest in keeping a diary, maybe get a stress ball, anything to help you vent without being destructive. I'm also going to give you a little medication to help with your feelings until things aren't so overwhelming for you."

"Medicine? I'm just sad I don't think I really need any type of medication," I protest.

"Alyssa, you're stealing, sneaking out of your house at night and venting your anger in destructive ways. It is my job to set up some precautions to help make sure that these unhealthy behaviors don't escalate. This medicine will help, but I need your commitment. Do you have any ideas on how you're going to handle your emotions from now on?" he asks.

I draw a blank. I don't have too many hobbies and normally I'd vent all of my problems to Shana, but now she's dead.

"Do you have something you enjoy doing with your spare time? Do you like to read, or write? Maybe some art?" he suggests.

"I play guitar?" I answer.

He nods. "Well, why don't you practice writing some new songs on your guitar when you're feeling down?"

"I- I'll give it a shot," I answer.

He writes some things down. "Alright, I'm going to hand this prescription over to your parents, and I'm going to give you my card. I hear you're going to Michigan, but I will need you to call and follow up with me every week okay?" he asks. I nod. He gets up and leaves the room.

As the door opens I can hear a hysterical woman. It's Mrs. Hawthorn. I put my hands to my face, listening to her cries. She's begging the police to find out who did this to Shana. As her pain radiates out, I can feel it. She's lost both of her children, all her family has worked for. Her dream was to raise her kids, send them off to college, and then retire with her husband. Now she has no children, and wants whoever is responsible- the fiend, to pay. I can't blame her, but as her cries hit me, I feel his presence. It's here to either stalk me or revel in her pain- probably both.

"Just go away. You've done enough damage. Just leave us alone," I mutter under my breath, so quietly that I can barely hear my own voice.

Sheriff Fraser enters.

"Time to go," he says.

I look at him. "Go?" I ask.

"You're free to go." I slowly rise to my feet and begin to walk out.

As I approach him, he gives me a sincere look. "I'm sorry for your loss. We are doing everything we can to put an end to this. I want to thank you. You've given us some hope that the rest of the missing children may be alive. We aren't going to stop looking until we find each and every one of them, and put the crook behind bars. I need you to stay strong, and be careful."

His words ring in my ears. How many times have people tried to comfort me? There's Bubbe, the doctor, my mom... It's like everyone is counting on me, but no matter what the police do, the only way they'll get the children back is to pull them from the shadow world. The only reason I was able to get Shana back was because I hacked off that totem-branch and then pulled her out myself. Maybe if that tree gets cut down they'll stop other kids from being kidnapped, but I doubt that would bring the ones already taken back. Even when I removed the branch I still had to manually pull Shana from the shadow world. The sheriff is wasting his time.

17: The Reprisal

I strum a few notes on my guitar. I'm sitting on my bed, waiting. I'm at least humoring Doctor Filbert by trying my guitar, though I don't know what good it will do seeing as he doesn't know the truth of the story. I don't know what I'm waiting for, maybe I'm just trying to pass the time.

We aren't going to make it to Michigan today. After what happened my parents are trying to help the Hawthorns. I'm not sure what they plan on doing to help, aside from keeping them company by sitting shivah with them, but they're worried that with the confirmed death of their last daughter, that they might just give up and end their own lives. That's why they didn't let Adam or me go with them…they figured there is no need to flaunt their two still-present children in the Hawthorns' faces.

When that thought plays through my head I pluck another note. I feel the loss of Shana too though. I play another. I feel the static presence, but refuse to look around for it. I guess he's playing the waiting game too.

What's he waiting for though? Is he waiting for me to fall asleep, does he just want to watch me, or am I still releasing enough pain for it feed on? I play a third note. I can imagine what he's doing to the others he has captive right now. He's probably causing them pain so he can feed off of them. I hardly care about Jason and Leanne. Call me hateful, but there are people I actually do have reason to worry about, like the five year old Lionel. Can he even comprehend what's going on?

I play the first note again, and realize that the three notes make a tune I recognize, but I can't name it. I keep playing, one note at a time. Each note seems dark, and hangs in the air, not even having fully played out before the next note. I know this song, but why can't I name it? It's very common. The pain has blocked out some of my memories and I'm having trouble pulling them out of my head. I keep playing each now with every ounce of concentration I can muster.

I can still sense the static in the background, but I ignore it. He can sit there and wait all he wants, I'm playing music. Maybe this is what the doctor meant. As I play this tune, I feel apathetic about the shadow's presence, and I'm so focused on playing the music that my thoughts are not even lingering on Shana. I still feel hurt, heartbroken, and scared, but with this guitar, I can push it all behind me. If only I can remember the name of it!

"Moonlight Sonata," says a voice. I look up and see Bubbe standing in the doorway. "It's been years since I've heard that song," she says.

"Moonlight Sonata," I repeat. It's one of the first songs I successfully learned. Why couldn't I remember it?

Bubbe sits on the bed next to me. She has a bottle of pills in her hand.

"Your Mom asked me to remind you to take these," she says. I look at the bottle.

"Prozac," I say aloud. I look her in the eye, asking if I should even bother taking them with a single gaze.

"I've never taken it before, but it might help you. If it's supposed to help with depression, then maybe it will help with your loss for a while, make it harder for him to get to you?" she suggests.

"My guitar is doing that right now," I say, resuming the song.

"Then maybe you should take these only when you are going to sleep...or when you're about to be a hero again?" she says. I chuckle a bit.

"Shana is the only one of them I'd ever do th-" I stop the sentence, listening to how cruel and selfish I sound. It may not be selfish to use that reasoning to refuse from going through the peril of the shadow world, but saying it aloud, when there are little kids suffering from his grasp just makes me sound evil.

"That's a smart thing though," she says. I look at her.

"Only risk your life to help the people you can't live without, like your family. You may mourn the loss of your classmates, but it's not worth subjecting yourself to him just out of compassion for them," she explains. I nod, she's right. I couldn't live without at least trying to help Shana, but as much as it sickens me to say this, I can live without Lionel Willow.

Bubbe and I sit here quietly while I play Moonlight Sonata. As sad and dark as the song sounds, it actually feels like it's alleviating the pain. I feel like all the sorrow that is inside of me, making me feel like I'm crawling out of my skin is just flowing out of me. Doctor Filbert is creepy and annoying, but he knows a little about letting go of pain and anger-without destroying things.

I can't believe how long it's been since I picked up my guitar. I missed it.

"So, when we go to Michigan, what happens then? Do we just stay there until he leaves?" I ask.

She shakes her head. "We might have to move," she answers.

"I don't know if he ever truly leaves one of his totems."

"But you said that there was a tree like it in Poland."

"There is, or at least there was. That doesn't mean he only has one feeding ground. He can probably go anywhere he pleases, but once he establishes a totem in an area, he has a permanent gateway there so he's probably going to drain that place dry and then keep watch."

I bow my head, thinking of another song to play. The thought that this- my home, now belongs to some fiend sickens me. Is there no way to defeat him? He's not of this world, that's for sure, but there's got to be something that will at least drive him away. I feel the static pulse. It's as if he can hear my thoughts, and is laughing at them. I play the first guitar chord that comes into mind and drown it out. Now I'm playing Denise's favorite song 'Complicated.'

"I always hated this song," says Bubbe.

I stop playing it and look at her with surprise. "I love Avril Lavigne!" I object.

"Oh, I just think this generation has better music is all." She looks up and around my various posters.

"Jimmy Eat World. That's a nice name. It's odd but nice," she says. I laugh at her a bit, and then I realize what she's doing. She's cheering me up, much like my parents are trying to do with the Hawthorns. Is Bubbe worried that I'm suicidal, or is she worried that I will do something stupid?

I play music all afternoon, ignoring the ominous presence of the entity. Sometimes I end up crying- or at least feel tears threatening to spill over, but as I do, I feel like I'm getting stronger. I feel like the pain is leaving. The thought that Shana is at peace instead of being tortured both hurts and helps me. I think maybe I accepted that I wasn't getting Shana back when she first disappeared, and that helped to dull the lingering pain of when she died. I'd already mourned her once. It didn't help with the shock of seeing her die though. That feeling of near triumph, only to fail, it's like I really did get dragged back to defeat at the edge of freedom, only not in the way I expected.

Our parents return, but even when they do, the house is quiet except for my music. I can't believe how long I've been able to keep this up. By the time I smell dinner, the joints of my fingers feel as if they're about to crack and my fingertips burn with wear. I still feel stronger though. It's as if every hour I play music the fiend's grip weakens.

Will I be able to keep this up tomorrow? No, tomorrow I should be even stronger. I should paint my nails, bleach my hair, and try to be normal. I'll look like a normal happy teenager ready to conquer the universe when I arrive in Michigan. Shana would want me to.

A smile crosses my lips as I head downstairs for dinner, which is very quiet today. There's a lot to talk about, but no one is really up to it. Bubbe and I have already said what we need to say, and I can sense mixed feelings about my actions coming from my parents. For one, they are horrified that I would venture off into the woods when there's a kidnapper on the loose, and yet I found Shana. I did something that all of the policemen and volunteers couldn't. I feel like I've downed at least three pounds of the spaghetti Mom has made before finally, she speaks up.

"The next flight isn't until nine P.M tomorrow so you'll be arriving in Michigan pretty late."

I've got more than twenty-four hours to wait before we get to safety? That blows. I guess maybe I'll try to sleep in. I wonder if Prozac will make me sleepy.

"Not planning on running off tonight are you?" she asks, half-jokingly.

I shake my head.

"Of course not," but I'm dead serious. The monster is probably waiting until I fall asleep so he can suck me back into his world. He'll probably try to lure me out with Shana or Lionel or something, but I won't let him. No, from now until nine tomorrow night I don't plan on setting foot out of this house. I don't care if he sits on the bed next to me.

After dinner I help clean up, bathe, and then get into some pajamas. It's been a restless day and I'm ready to turn in early, but I decide I will hold off another hour by cleaning my room a bit. I put all of the clothes strewn about the floor in the laundry bag. Mom will be horrified, but hopefully I won't be here to hear her when she sees it.

I throw CD's, books, and all of my scattered objects in places where they belong, just with no particular order. Oh well, I don't think I'll need to dig around for any of these CD's anytime soon since every one of these songs are already on my computer and mp3 player. Cleaning up is really helping to keep my mind off of Shana's death. It's going to be sad though, because unless they find some miraculous reason for me to return in time, I'm going to miss Shana's funeral. Me! Her best friend!

It's only when I'm finally done distracting myself that I fully take in the thought that even though I've saved her, I still miss her, and I'm always going to. Would it be worth it for me to come back for her funeral? Surely the Hawthorns will invite me? I shake off the thought. Now is not the time. Just before I climb in bed I am greeted by a loud static wave that almost knocks me over. "What was that?" I ask aloud.

The Slender Man

I can hear a steady flow of static erupting around the room. What's he planning? My heart sinks. No, no he's just trying to scare me. I carry on as if nothing happens, except I don't turn off my light. *He seems stronger*, I think to myself. He probably *is* going to try and lure me out tonight, and if that wave is any indication of his persistence, it probably means I'll have to deal with terrifying images that will be hard to ignore. I won't let him lure me, no matter what.

I pop two Prozac tablets into my mouth before lying down. I'm not sure what the proper dosage is for these pills. I think I remember seeing both one and two on the bottle. Maybe it's one during the day, two at night, or was it one tablet, twice a day, not to exceed two tablets in twelve hours? I'll live either way. I pull the blanket over my head to block out the light and slowly, but surely, I drift off.

I dream for a little while before waking up. I listen for the static, but it's not present. *Huh*, I think. Maybe I should get up and check? No, I try and go back to sleep, but that seems to be out of the question. As if waiting for me, I feel the static slowly creep on me and impulsively try to jump up before realizing that I can't move. *The paralysis again, it's going to try and pull me into the realm.* I don't feel the energy to fight it, but if I don't resist, then I will be sucked in and have to run out of his domain.

I hear a scream in the distance. It sounds like-it's Adam. I hear Adam screaming. It's not the same painful, ear-stabbing scream the Shana gave me when the fiend had her in the first nightmare; it's the sound of horrified surprise, like something is jumping out at him. He continues yelling and then I hear *him*.

"Help! Mom, Dad! Alyssa!" he screams. I feel the static grip tighten. No! I should have gotten up. He's going to get Adam. Wait a second, this is his trick. He's trying to weaken me by impersonating Adam. It's what he did to Shana, Jason, and probably the others. This won't work on me. I try and laugh, and although my voice is blocked by his grip, I can still exhale in rhythm. *'This won't work on me. I know what you're trying to do,'* I mouth while thinking it, hoping he understands what I'm saying.

"Help! Please!" Adam drags on, but I just laugh. I'm not falling for it. I prepared for this. I even took my medicine to help. Adam's screams are so real, but as I laugh at them, they get farther and farther away, and the fiend's grip weakens. *I've beaten you!* I think triumphantly.

No, I can say it now. Its grip is weak!

"I've beaten you. Na na-na na-na-na, you lose," I mumble childishly. When his presence fully disperses, I fall asleep with a smile on my face. A few hours later, I wake up. I feel like the medicine has worn off and feel a sour taste in my mouth.

"Forgot to brush," I mumble.

I climb out of bed and head to the bathroom to brush my teeth. It's pretty early, but I figure I will go back to sleep for another six hours or so. As I brush my teeth I remember my little run-in with the entity earlier. I don't feel amused this time. Maybe I'm too groggy for it, but I decide I'll check in on Adam before I go back to bed. I rinse and then head over to Adam's room.

His window is open and so it's freezing in here, but it's almost always open so that's not what catches my attention. On the floor is the sling for Adam's cast. I don't see him dropping it by himself, and then not picking it back up. His bed is empty. Did it really get him?

"Adam!" I shout. There's no way. "Adam!" I scream.

"Adam!"

18: The Message

No matter what I do, that monster- he's always one step ahead of me. I finally thought I had him figured out. We just had to get through one more night and day, and I was ready to handle it, but he saw right through me. He has his own stage set up, and I have no say in what happens. In the middle of the night, when I thought he was trying to lure me out, he wasn't. He just wanted me to listen while he hurt and kidnapped my brother. He wanted me to try and get up and come to his aid, only to be held back. He got Adam, and he made me listen to it. Maybe I would have figured that out if I wasn't on the medication.

No, if not for the medication I'd only have been more emotionally tortured by Adam's cries. Now I sit, half of my body against the wall, as the police- whom I must have seen a hundred times this week already- get their answers. Of course we have none for them. Adam is just another missing child to add to their list. He's just another one of the children they need to find, but never will. I'm not crying, and there are no tears. I'm just sitting here listening to the footsteps, cries, and words of those around me. The sheriff isn't here yet, but Deputy Yew is.

Why couldn't he- the monster, just let us go? There are other kids for him to take still, but he had to come after Adam and me. What makes us so special? Is it that we've already fed him so much pain that he wants to milk us for everything we have? I don't know. Maybe he was irritated that I was recovering so quickly instead of giving in to hopelessness in the face of loss.

There's got to be something I can do about Adam. Shana is one person I thought I couldn't live without, but Adam... Adam is helpless. He's seven, weakened, and traumatized by watching the death of his friends. I recall how much pain and how scared I felt when I was in that realm. How is someone in Adam's condition handling it? I can't let him suffer like that. I have to do something about it. Can I go back in and get him out? That axe is probably still on the ground somewhere, but he was watching and waiting for me before. He'll probably intercept me more quickly from the start.

Even if I do make it to the tree, there's no way I can repeat the process I did with Shana. I was barely able to escape with her assistance that time.

I feel the sounds of those around me drown out, covered by a new sound. It's him. I turn around and look. Out of my peripheral vision, I catch him standing in the hallway. I can't look any closer without having my eyes sting. Has he come for me now? No, he's just here to rub it in and enjoy the fruits of his evil. The adults are downstairs, and even if they were up here with me, they'd be oblivious to him. I look in my hand at Adam's sling. I've been holding it for a while now. This won't be my last memory of him. I toss the sling in the fiend's direction not even looking to see if it passes right through him, or if he blocks its course.

"I want him back," I mutter aloud. I close my eyes, expecting him to laugh, but he just waits there. I do my best to hide my emotions, both inside and out, but I'm not sure it's working. Maybe I should take another Prozac? No, that would mean walking right by him to get it, and I can only imagine what will happen if I risk that. I sit here, quietly, almost catatonic for a long time. It could be hours, or maybe it's only been thirty minutes. All I know is I felt a few pats on my shoulder, hugs, and the police are gone.

I can hear my parents having hysterical conversations on their phones. They must be notifying our relatives of Adam's disappearance. Maybe they're looking to receive condolences for Adam to help comfort themselves, but in my opinion that only makes more people feel bad. It's justifiable though. The way I feel about Adam... I need a friend to convey my feelings as well; I need Shana, but he's taken her as well.

He's taken too much from me. He's taken my family, friends, health, and social life. He may not have me in his shadowy prison, but he's feeding off me nonetheless. I feel an arm around my shoulder and see that Bubbe has assumed a sitting position next to me. She doesn't say anything, but I can tell she feels the same way about Adam as I do, and knows exactly what I do about his disappearance. Our feelings are mutual, and there's hardly anything to say.

"He's here, waiting for me," I say.

"I know."

"He wants me next."

"I know," she answers.

"What do I do? I can't leave for Michigan without him. I won't."

"I don't know."

That's all we can bother to say. There's no use wasting words, but from what I have said, I know one thing is true. I can't leave without Adam. I won't let myself, and if it means I have to try and pull off the same rescue attempt I did for Shana- at the cost of my life, then I'll try. Even if he dies in my arms like she did, I won't let the fiend keep him.

"We can't sit here like this. It only encourages him," she says.

"So what do we do? Ignore him like nothing happened?" I ask, horrified at the thought of- not thinking.

She shakes her head. "We'll think of something, but he's only feeding off of us when we're like this," she says.

More tears come from my eyes. I slowly stand up, unsure of what I am going to do. I sense the static, but the monster isn't in the hallway right now. He's stalking from somewhere else. Despite it being her own advice, Bubbe doesn't appear ready to get up quite yet. I walk over into my room, wondering if I'll see him waiting, but I can only sense him. Maybe he really is in here, but is standing just on the other side of the veil that separates our worlds-and is just not visible at the moment. He could be right in front of me at this very moment and I wouldn't know it.

I look around the room for something to do. Maybe I should play my guitar, and take some medication. Medication could help keep my emotions in check. I walk over to my nightstand and pick up the bottle of Prozac. I screw open the top, but when I feel the lid open, I stop. Is this what I've resorted to, drugs to keep me sane while the fiend watches me? I feel a sudden surge inside my chest.

I'm not sure where it's coming from, but it feels like I'm imploding. I'm squeezing the medicine bottle so hard that my nails are digging into my palm. I feel a surge of rage, fear, and anguish all hit me at once.

"Why!?" I scream at the top of my lungs. I turn and throw the bottle as hard as I can. It hits my vanity mirror and scatters pills across my room, leaving a crack in the glass, but I don't care. I don't care for vanity. I don't care for health. I don't care for the police. I don't care for myself. I want Adam back.

I kick my suitcase, causing its contents to spill out over the floor. I pick up bottles of nail polish and throw them, on the floor; at the walls; everywhere. I scream again, this time it's mostly anger coming from my throat. My vision blurs. I throw something else. I'm not sure what it is, maybe a shoe, and I hear more glass breaking in response. I throw everything I can get my hands on, not paying any attention whatsoever to where they land.

Every time I throw something, I scream.

"It's not fair!" *Slam.*

"I didn't do anything to deserve this!" *Bang.*

"Just leave us alone!" I rip autographed posters from my wall. I rip my blankets from my bed. I tear out the contents of my closet, trying to find more objects to throw. "Show your face!" I scream.

"Alyssa!" I feel arms wrap around me. I squirm and push, but I can't get out.

"Calm down!" I hear Dad shout. It takes me a second to realize that he's the one that has me.

"Oh my god," Mom exclaims. I don't understand exactly what's happening. I have my head in my hands, and I'm sitting against something. I hear the static again, and this time it's doing that rhythmic pulsing. He's laughing at me. It takes all I can to keep from clawing my nails down my face. I hear Mom on the phone, and from the conversation she's having I can assert that she's speaking with Doctor Filbert. I guess I'm bound from the nearest psychiatric ward soon, a perfect place to go crazy in.

"You should take a bath. We're going to see your Doctor," I hear Dad.

"I don't need a shrink," I say.

"Have you seen your room? Have you seen yourself!?" he shouts.

"Honey," Mom interjects. "Listen, we want to find Adam just as much as you do. You forget that we love him too, but we love you as well. We need to be together in this, and we can't have you being destructive."

"It's not that big a deal. Just a tantrum," I say.

The Slender Man

"Just a tantrum? You've smashed hundreds of dollars' worth of your stuff in your 'just a tantrum'," argues Dad.

"Lyss, some of that stuff in there you cherished. You would scream at us if we leaned against your signed posters or when we touched one of your pictures. You've destroyed all of that now. We're worried."

"And your vanity. Practically brand new," Dad mutters under his breath, although he's way off in that case. I hear what they're saying, but all of that seems petty compared to Adam.

"Just take a bath, and get the nail polish out of your hair," Mom says.

"We'll never get the nail polish out of these clothes. All trash," grunts Dad.

I get up and head over to the bathroom, grabbing a towel on the way. I turn the hot water on and flip the switch to keep it from draining. While the bath is running I look at myself in the mirror. I'm surprised at myself. Although I don't feel it, I can see why my parents are worried. There is what seems like a gallon of nail polish splashed across my body. Some of it is clotting my hair together and my clothes... at least they're night clothes. There's no way I'll get all of this cleaned up in a single bath, and right now I really don't care to.

I stop the water, undress, and climb in. I draw the curtain and lay my head to rest against the edge of the tub even though my face and hair have the most nail polish damage, and will be the most difficult to clean. The hot water burns my skin a little, but it's soothing as well. I just rest here, letting the hot water calm me down. I hope they're not expecting me to finish quickly.

What have I done though? Not to my room, but to Adam. Is there some way I could have avoided this? Is there some drastic turn of events I caused that led to this? If I hadn't gotten up to rescue Shana, we'd be in Michigan already. We'd be safe, but then I'd spend my whole life wondering if I could have saved her, and now that I have tried, I'm going to spend my whole life regretting Adam's disappearance. Whether I live to be an old woman, or if I die trying to get him back, it's never going to go away.

I lay my head back, adjusting my position in the water. I close my eyes and breathe deep, and exhale in a sorrowful sigh.

"I'll never find peace, will I?" I ask myself. I rest here for a few more seconds, trying to harvest whatever peace I can get, when I have a very unwelcome guest.

"Go away," I cry as the static appears. My voice is already cracked and I can feel the tears coming. *Stop crying damnit*! I tell myself. It's just what he wants.

The Slender Man

I open my eyes and turn my head to the side. He's here, just inside the door. I can see his silhouette outside the shower curtain. His black, slim form rendered imperfectly still by his jagged contortions. "Why?" I ask.

No response.

"What have I done to deserve this?"

He just stands there.

"Give him back."

Nothing.

"Please," I cry, but still nothing. I am about to turn away from him, when he starts moving- really moving. I watch as he leans over, and I almost think his eye-searing head is going to peek over the shower curtain, when I see more limbs come from him.

These are identical to his arms that come down below the bathtub rim, except they extend from his back. What is he doing? I wonder. Suddenly his form shrinks until it's normal human size aside from his arms and tendrils. I hear laughter. I recognize the voice.

"Jason," I say aloud.

"You aren't as strong as you think," he says. His figure morphs again. Why do I hear Jason?

"You don't deserve to be freed from this!" shouts Leanne angrily. He can mimic Leanne too?

"Stop," I cry, but his figure morphs.

"Why didn't you save him? You rescued your friend instead of my brother. My five-year-old brother. Don't you think he deserves to be saved?" accuses Lindsay. Lindsay is gone too? Why haven't I heard about this? He must have taken her recently, or maybe the police just didn't relay it to us due to our own troubles.

"Please stop," I cry, but he morphs again.

"Alyssa... why won't you help me? You helped Shana, but I'm your brother. You won't help me?" asks Adam in a pleading tone. That one hits home and I can't help but cry loudly.

"Why are you doing this to me?" I say. "Give him back to me," I beg.

"Give him back and I'll come. I'm stronger than him. I'll last longer. Just let him go and I'll come," I offer hysterically. I see Adam's long and slender hand reach out and through the curtain. I grab it and am greeted by a wave of static, but I don't care. I just want Adam back. I climb to my knees and clasp both of my hands around Adam- or the fiend's.

"Just let him go. Just let him go," I repeat over and over.

The hand jerks away and I look back to see the fiend returning to his normal form. He's not laughing like I expect him to be, instead he seems menacing. He's assuming a posture that implies that he's about to attack. Is he going to take me? If he does will he give back Adam? I feel a surge of the static screech, and I close my eyes in response. I can't breathe. I flail and struggle but something is wrong. I feel consciousness slipping. He's killing me. No, I want to see Adam freed first.

"No…" I try and scream, but it's distorted, and I can't draw the breath to continue. I lose control and panic. I open my eyes again and notice something. I'm underwater. I thrust myself up and have to cough water out before being able to gaspingly draw a much needed breath.

Was it just a dream? No this entity works with dreams. He's a living nightmare. What just happened was him at work. Maybe I fell asleep when I closed my eyes, and slipped underwater, or maybe he forced me into a trance. I don't know, but I hurry up and do what I came here for and scrub as much nail polish off my skin as I can. I have to use my nails to pull it off my skin, and by the time I get it all off my skin is red and tender from the scratching.

When I finish I climb out and look around at the water mess I made when flailing about. How could my parents not come to my aid when they heard that commotion, unless the monster masked it somehow? I notice in the steamy mirror that I've missed a few spots particularly in the hair area, but I let it go. I ponder the dream I just had.

"What do I do?" I ask myself. There's a knock on the door.

"Alyssa, the sheriff wants to talk to you," says Mom.

"The sheriff?" I ask.

"Yes he says it's important. Will you hurry up? He's on the phone," she says.

"Alright." Instead of blow drying my hair I wrap a towel around it and walk out of the bathroom. Garbed in nothing but two towels I take the phone from Mom and head down the hall to my room. I almost faint when I look at the damage I caused. No wonder my parents freaked.

"H-Hello?" I answer the phone, realizing the sheriff is still waiting.

"This Alyssa Redwood?" asks Sheriff Fraser.

"Yes sir," I answer.

"I have some news. It may be good or bad, but it involves you."

"Uh-huh?"

"We found Mario Douglas," he says.

"The bus driver?"

"Yeah, one of our men arrested him outside the woods. Listen he doesn't seem to be himself, and he keeps saying your name. We want to bring you down here and see if maybe he'll give you some answers. If he's just jabbering on, well, it can't hurt. Would you be willing to talk with him for us?" he asks.

The Slender Man

"Well yeah. I mean if my parents are okay with it," I answer.

"I already ran it by your Mom. She said you may not be feeling up for it," he says.

"Oh no, that was- something else."

"Alright then. We'll see you soon," he says.

Mom is standing in the hallway. She doesn't say anything, but I can tell she heard my end of the conversation.

"I'll be ready in ten," I say. It takes me a while to find a matching set of clothes among the torn and broken hangers in my closet, and it's not that I'm being picky, it's that I threw a really big tantrum. I'm somewhat embarrassed, or at least I would be if there weren't so many more important things to be upset over. I settle on white tank top some jeans and a jacket. I put my socks and sneakers on and brush my hair out so it's detangled, if still messy. I'll deal with it.

I leave everything else, not even sure if there's anything I still have that I can put on, seeing as I probably destroyed every cosmetic item I own. It looks like Dad isn't coming. He's in the living room chair with a half-empty bottle of Shabbat wine next to him. He's not a heavy drinker so he's probably drunk himself unconscious by now. If only I could escape with sleep...

Mom, Bubbe, and I all head out single file to the car. I look around, but don't see, or even sense the entity. For some reason he's dropped his 'round-the-clock watch on me. The drive to the police station is quiet, but full of tension. My thoughts are focused on Adam and Adam only, and by the time we get to the station, it takes me a second to remember why I'm coming here, Mr. Mario. Maybe he has some answers for me. If the fiend really did have him, and he's out now looking for me... well this has to help me in some way right?

Deputy Yew, grim as ever, is waiting for us outside the station. He nods when we walk up the steps and guides us in. When we enter the station, there are over a dozen eyes on me. Some of them are giving me quizzical looks, and others confused. Some are sympathetic, and others have hopeful gazes. I think I even catch a few accusing glares, as if Mario looking for me means I'm involved in some way. Regardless, everyone including me wants answers.

Deputy Yew leads us back to the jail area. The metal detectors go off when he walks through, and even when I walk through, probably because of my belt, but no one stops me. It's not the time for formalities. We get down to the jail cells, and the single occupant waits in the cell furthest from us. I feel that I can't walk fast enough to get the answers I want, but I don't want to run. When I get to the cell, I see Mario hunched like Gollum on his bed. "Mr. Mario," I say. He looks up.

The Slender Man

"...Redwood. Alyssa Redwood," he says as though he'd already been saying it. He locks eyes with me for a moment and stops speaking. He's still in his hospital gown, although by now it's torn and dirty, and he seems to have aged ten years since I last saw him. His gaze fades from crazed to angry. "Only, Alyssa," he says, pausing between the words.

Deputy Yew gives me a quick look to make sure I'm okay with it. I nod at him. He in turn nods to the sheriff and they escort my confused mother and Bubbe out of the holding area. Deputy Yew stops down the hall a little way to at least provide supervision while giving as much privacy as possible, and it looks like that works for Mario too.

"Alyssa," says Mr. Mario.

"What happened to you?" I ask. He looks down at the ground and suddenly his face turns into the saddest child face I've ever seen. He starts crying a bit.

"I don't know," he mutters.

"You don't know, Mr. Mario? The accident? You were missing from the hospital." If he doesn't remember, then maybe he won't have any answers for me.

"I don't know. I don't know. I don't know," he mutters. I'm starting to feel a little disappointment, but I try a different approach.

"Why did you ask to speak with me?" I ask. He pauses his crying, as if remembering something.

"He told me to," he answers.

"He? Who is he?" I ask, although I know who he's talking about.

"The Slender… he's the Slender Man. He told me to. He let me go to tell you," he answers. *Slender Man?* I think. Is that really his name, or what we call him? It certainly fits.

"Why? What does…*Slender* want?" I ask, dubbing him with a nickname. "What does he want you to tell me?"

He rocks back and forth a bit. "He has your Adam," he says.

"I know, but will he give him back? Will he give my b- my Adam back?" I ask.

He shakes his head.

"He's mad at you. You shouldn't have left. You've, angered him," he says. I try to think of the best thing to say next, but he continues. "You stole from him, so he stole from you."

"He let you go to tell me that?" I ask. "What does he want now?"

"He wants you. Only you. You stole from him. Now he wants you."

"But he already wanted me, and Adam! He already tried to pull me in and-"

"But you escaped!" he interrupts loudly. I can see Deputy Yew about to rush over but I hold out my palm. "You won't escape again," he continues. "What if I leave? He won't have me then," I bluff.

Mr. Mario starts laughing, and then starts crying. "He's not going to let you go. He'll follow you."

"But what about Adam? If I let him take me will he give back Adam?" I ask quietly as to not alarm Deputy Yew.

Mr. Mario ponders the situation.

"He wants you to come to him. If you don't come to him, he'll take you," he says.

"That's his message? Come to him or he'll take me by force? What happens if I come of my own will?" I ask, leaning against the bars.

He slowly gets up and walks over to me. His face six inches from mine, he says.

"He wants to play a game. If you come to him... he'll play nice. If you run from him..." He stops and walks back. "If you run from him," he tries again, but he puts his hands to face.

"Don't run from him. If you run then both of you will suffer... worse," he explains. He crawls into the fetal position on the floor.

I look away, considering what he's just told me. Does... *Slender* want a rematch? What does he mean by game? Is he just going to toy with me and then capture me? How can I trust him? I can trust that he'll follow me. That's one thing, but he wants me to come to him willingly... again? Does this mean I'm doomed?

"I just want to see my brother again," I say, more to myself then Mr. Mario.

"He'll be there. The Slender Man has him. He'll always be there," says Mr. Mario.

"How do I bring him back?" I ask.

"How do I bring my brother out of that world without killing him? Do I cut a branch from the tree? Or...?" I ask.

He looks up at me forlornly, as if he's calculating whether not he should answer me, whether or not he's *allowed* to. Finally he speaks.

"The Slender Man... he gains control by hurting and breeding pain. He feeds on the suffering of his victims. He feeds on misery and pain... So bring him joy, and life," he says quietly.

Joy and life? I ponder. I hear static creeping up on me. It starts off quietly, but then I hear Mario screaming loudly and convulsing on the floor. He's flailing wildly, but even though I know what's torturing him, I can't see it. I step back as Deputy Yew rushes to unlock the cell and get inside. By the time he does, Sheriff Fraser and another officer have already caught up. The static disperses as they reach Mario.

"Get me some paramedics!" shouts Sheriff Fraser.

The Slender Man

Deputy Yew, thumb on Mr. Mario's wrist shakes his head.

"He's dead."

19: The Walk

Mr. Mario doesn't deserve what happened to him. Slender killed him, but the police think he may have had a heart attack. They'll have to wait for a coroner's report. The look on Mario's face shows me that it was no natural heart attack though. He was scared to death. He couldn't remember who he was or what he did. All he could remember was the Slender Man, and my name. He probably didn't even know who I was, but he gave up what little life he had left to give me a bit of helpful information. I'll be sure to go to his funeral, if I survive that is.

Now I'm sitting at home in Bubbe's room. Bubbe talked Mom into waiting until tomorrow to take me to see Doctor Filbert, and I don't even think

The Slender Man

Dad's awake yet. I've just told Bubbe what Mr. Mario told me. She shakes her head.

"I knew something was wrong, from the moment you jumped in the hospital," she says.

"I saw him then, and it was obvious that you had too, but I didn't say anything. I dismissed it like some village idiot, and now it's gone this far. He's taken Adam, and now he wants you." I hold her hand.

"There are things I could have done differently too Bubbe, but I didn't," I say. There are tears coming from her eyes, the first real tears I've seen from her in a while.

"If we'd have gotten out of here sooner... I can't help but think we'd be okay. Maybe not that poor girl Shana, oh no we couldn't have left her, but if we'd gotten you to safety immediately. I should have known- I did know, but I didn't say anything, and I'm sorry for that," she continues.

I can't let her blame herself for this, not at her age.

"Bubbe, I'm going to do something about this. Mr. Mario, just before he died he said to bring joy and happiness to weaken Slender's hold. It had to have meant something because Slender killed him right after, like a punishment or to keep him from telling me more, but what does that mean? Do I literally have to go to him joyous and happy?" I ask.

She thinks for a moment, but I don't think she's composing a wise answer to my question. I think she's lingering on the fact that I'm planning to go out there. "Bubbe, I have to. I told you what Mario said. I've been marked ever since I escaped his world the first time, and now he's angry. If I go to him now I may have a chance to retrieve Adam, and if I don't it will just be worse for both of us."

"I know that! Don't you think I know that, child? I don't want to hear it anymore though. You can't expect to reason with pain when reasoning won't help," she cries. I haven't heard Bubbe actually yell like that in years. I only hope Mom didn't hear it, because I bet she hasn't either. Bubbe bows her head.

"Joy and life... it makes sense because if he feeds on pain and breeds death, he is no friend to life," she says.

"But what does that mean for me? I can't go in with a smile on my face, at least not an honest one." She looks up at me.

"But what makes you feel joy, laughter, and full of life? And what brings those feelings to Adam. What do you have in common?" she asks.

I can't tell if she's hinting at the answer, or if she's thinking aloud, hoping I will find an answer. What brings me joy? I remember painting my nails with Shana. That brought me happiness, but when she disappeared I didn't have anything. All I had was "...my guitar," I say aloud.

"Your guitar," Bubbe repeats.

"His favorite song is the prayer Adon Olam. The upbeat, happy tune to that song always brought a smile to his face. Even when he was sick, or upset, he always loved that song."

I nod slowly.

"That's why I always played it. You don't think…"

"I think it's the best answer we've got so far," she says.

"But last time I don't even remember having the axe when he pulled me in, how will a guitar make it through?"

"It might, but at any rate he didn't take your voice did he?" she asks. I shake my head.

"I think if you play your heart out on your guitar and sing your brother that song- I think that might be the only joy and life that passes through to his shadow world."

I feel my stomach churn as the memories of the last time I was there come to me. I keep dwelling on the idea that I won't succeed, and that I won't even make it there, but now he's practically- no he's literally invited me to come in. He's insisted that I come of my own accord. I bet now I could walk up with a chainsaw and he wouldn't hurt me till I reach the tree. I doubt it would do me any good though. "When, when do I do it?" I ask.

She looks out her window at the night sky.

"I don't think he's going to let you sleep through the night," she says, brutally honest.

"Alright then," I say, voice cracking. I hate the idea of going back out there, but not as much as I hate the idea of leaving Adam there to suffer. I hate everything right now, and I especially hate the fact that I can't even cry it out, because that will only help him. His static presence rings through my ears. He's probably overheard our entire conversation. He probably hears every thought coursing through my mind right now.

Bubbe stands up and I feel her hand on my shoulder. I look down and see she's holding something in her other hand, something I haven't seen until now.

"I found this thrown on your floor," she says. My eyes widen in shame as I see what's in her hand. It's the Star of David necklace she gave me, the one that's practically ancient treasure. She didn't even pass it down to Mom and here I am throwing it in the floor.

"I'm sorry, I-" I say, trying to apologize, but I silence myself as she clasps the necklace around my neck and hugs me. I hug her back tightly.

"I'm sorry you have to do this. I feel like it's my job to stop you, but I know there's no other way. I wish I could go in your stead, but just promise me something," she says.

"What?" I ask, crying.

"Don't make me lose both of my grandchildren," she orders. I nod.

"Alright good-"

"Don't say goodbye either, because you're coming back with Adam in your arms," she says.

I nod again. Right-O.

"What about Mom?" I ask.

"Didn't I say you were coming back?" she says. I laugh a bit.

"Go get your guitar."

I let go and slowly walk to my room, planning out my actions. Surely I'll at least get to see Adam while I'm in there, and all I should have to do is escape with Adam in my arms. If he wants me so badly, then he'll probably try to attack me instead of Adam if we run together. Last time I felt that he could only take one of us at a time, and he and I both know that I'm the one he wants. I pick up my guitar and take one long look at it. It's worn, but the light brown body is still very shiny, despite being completely covered in finger prints and smudges. I've only ever had to change the strings once.

I sling the guitar around my back and slowly creep downstairs. I can see Dad is still on his chair, and I see Mom's legs from around the corner, and a big blanket dangling to the floor. She must have crawled in with him, lights on and everything. I blow them a silent kiss and creep out the door. I shut it as quietly as I can behind me.

I walk down to the end of the driveway and turn around. This might be the last time I see my house. I take in the beige coloring and look up to see my broken window, but with the curtain you can't see inside my room. I guess that's how I didn't know it was broken until now.

I turn around and head straight for the woods. I only stop to go through my routine of stretches at the end of the sidewalk. I'm not planning on running in, but I bet there will be a lot of running involved in getting back out, and now would be the worst time of all to twist an ankle, although my stretches haven't prevented me from stumbling before. I take my time, and I can feel Slender's impatience with me. I get my hamstrings, quadriceps, and even my arms in twenty second counts. I wish I hadn't pick jeans to wear, because they will really limit my flexibility. *It's not too late to go back and change,* I think but shake it off. That's just a way to delay the inevitable.

I march into the woods, as confident as I can be. I'm not in very deep before the woods begin to get very dark, only moonlight guiding my path. I wonder if it will be darker in the shadow world, because at least there I have light radiating from my own body, although it grows dim very quickly when Slender has me.

As I find my way up the first slope I hear something in the distance. It's a scream. There's a girl screaming in pain. I shudder, and move on. I almost want to close my eyes but I won't be able to find my way to the tree if I do.

I hear another scream, it's coming from far behind me now. It's male this time, but I still don't recognize who it belongs to. Slender is trying to drop my morale. I won't let him. As I hear a third scream, this one ahead of me, I pull my guitar from my back. I have to walk more carefully as to not hit it against the trees, but it's worth it.

I pick a scale and repeat it. It's more of a string skipping exercise, but it keeps music in the air, and I don't have to worry too much about messing up the tab from a song. I keep playing the notes and then I hear another scream. I have to close my eyes for a few seconds at this one. It's so long and drawn out that I find myself playing random notes on all strings in order to drown it out. Lionel's cries of agony ring out. Slender knows this one is bothering the most, so he keeps playing it.

I have to play a song now, a happy one. I try to think of most of the music I listen to, but a particularly happy song seems to escape my mind at every corner. I flip through bands in my head. *Chevelle?* No. *Avril Lavigne?* No. *Paramore?* I can't find one. I know so many cheerful songs, but they seem to be blocked from my memory. It's as if he's in my head, making sure there's no joy. I'll fight it. I begin playing a random riff. I don't know if it's one I'm pulling from one of the forgotten songs lost in my subconscious, or if I'm making it up as I go along. All I know is it's a mellow, soft-acoustic song, and as I play it, I can barely hear the screams.

The screams play louder, no they're closer. Now it's both Lindsay and Lionel- brother and sister, screaming. I wonder if he's hurting them together. Does Lindsay have to watch her brother writhe in pain? I shake the thought by playing more loudly. *I'm almost there,* I tell myself in my mind, even though I've just barely crossed the halfway point. The screams are louder and more frequent, and it's as if I hear the screams of every child I've known him to take - excluding Shana and Adam.

Leanne and Jason ring out, followed by someone I don't recognize, followed by Lionel. Now he's so loud he is drowning out my guitar. I won't let him. I pluck the strings loudly and off-key, not with the intent of the song I'm playing, but just to mask the cries.

I reach the final slope, and the cries are cut off all at once. It's as if someone abruptly hit pause on a simultaneous screaming track. I don't hesitate, although I'm progressing slowly. I don't fully know what to expect, but as the tree comes into view, my heart fills with dread. I do the best I can to pull up anger, but I just don't have enough of it in my system. No! I *need* joy, I *have* to be joyous.

I reach the top of the hill. The tree has gotten much taller. It must be twenty-five feet in height, and not half a foot wide. I get where the term *Slender* originates. It still has those two low hanging branches that are almost as tall as the tree alone; the arms, and then the rest of the branches, all stemming from the back and all pointed up. There are more of these than there ever were before. I know that we are right-the branches are somehow representative of the children he takes, and Slender has been busy. I count fifteen branches now, not including the fallen one next to the axe on the ground.

I feel a continuous stream of static. With the static comes numbness, but slowly. I feel goose-bumps as shivers run through my body, but I pretend to not notice. I walk up to the tree, face to face, and I am about to play the guitar when I think of the boldest thing possible. I turn around with my eyes closed, and lean with my back against the tree. "Time to be happy Adam, I hope you're listening," I say.

I take a deep breath and force a smile, and then I begin playing the tab for Adon Olam. As I play I feel the static get closer. It's not necessarily stronger than before, but it feels closer. All of my muscles tense involuntarily. Is he right here? I slink down into a sitting position, still leaning on the tree. I feel something touch my arm. It's feels like a hand with long, slender fingers. It's coming from behind me. I shiver. I'm practically vibrating by this point, but I continue.

I begin singing in a tremulous voice.

"Adon... Olam..." I feel heavy fluid trickle down my nose. "...asher malach," I continue, but my body is starting to go numb. I feel another hand grab me gently, as if just to tease me, and the way the static is slowly pulsing, it's almost as if it's breathing down my neck instead of laughing. I take another breath, trying not to hyperventilate.

"b'terem kol... y'tzir nivra..." I mutter, but my voice cracks. *Stop being afraid. Don't be afraid damnit!* I keep playing,

"...L'et na'asah, v'cheftzo kol..." I feel unbearably drowsy as Slender's static aura engulfs me, pulling me through, burning.

"...azai melech, sh'mo nikra..." and I fall over... limp.

20: The Slender Man

Bump, bump, bump. I can hear my heartbeat. I can feel it. With each beat it gets heavier. I'm not dead, I know that much. He's sucked me in. I feel numbness penetrate my body and shudder in response, but it's no time to be scared. That's what he wants, but I came here expecting this. I already know what it's like in this shadow world. I hold myself still, waiting for Slender's screaming laughter, or the jagged pain, but neither come. I only hear my heartbeat, and static. What's happening?

I open my eyes, it's very dark, but the light coming from me is brighter than before. I still can't see anything outside of the clearing though. I see no sign of Adam, or the Slender Man. I lean forward, balancing my- *my guitar!* I still have it. Apparently I *can* bring things through. If only I smuggled Dad's shotgun in. If only a shotgun would work on this fiend.

I slowly make it to my feet, stumbling as I get used to the numbness. This has already happened to me twice before, you'd think I'd adjust more quickly by now, but it's like dipping into cold water; no matter how many times you experience it, you're never really prepared for the sensation.

I turn around to look at the tree. It's moving, but not contorting, and there's no black vortex-vein connecting me to it. Slender really must have special plans for me, but what does he want me to do? I take a few steps, unsure of which direction to turn. I'm starting to feel anxious, trying to anticipate what's going to happen next. He's going to jump out at me, or grab me suddenly. No, he must be expecting me to wander off with no guidance, to try and escape, and eventually fall into his trap, if I'm not trapped already.

"Adam!" I call, but my voice is muffled, as if this is a dream. I can still hear my voice. It just won't project into a shout. Is he blocking the sound then? I strum a chord on my guitar to see what's going on. I feel the vibrations pass through my body, and the sound of the guitar resonates for a while, but it's very discordant.

"Your move," I say, boldly.

The Slender Man

Slender must be taking the bait, because here's Leanne's scream. It's coming from my left, deeper into the woods. "Right," I say. He must want me to follow Leanne's calls. I do my best to not let fear overcome me, but I can hardly help myself. Every second I tell myself. "He wants me to be scared," in an effort to calm myself down, and it does, if only a little. I walk into the woods, every step showing me another leafless tree.

Leanne's screams get louder which means I'm getting closer. I walk for about another minute before I see Leanne lying on the ground. There is no light coming from her body, but she's moving a little bit. I stand above her, and watch her body distort. She's ghostly pale, and if not for her slight movements I would think she's dead. "Leanne?" She distorts again, and I jump back as the once-prone Leanne is now standing face-to-face with me inside one flash. She looks angry, but her eyes are blank, and her body is emitting this shadowy aura. What's worse is while she's standing like this, she is continuously distorting, and in between the flashes she seems to have no face, but when she does have a face it's set in that vengeful look, the hateful look I last saw her directing toward me.

I wait for her to make a move. She distorts again and now she's on her knees crying for help. Confronted with this pitiful version of her, I can't help but feel, well, pity. He's showing me that

Leanne is still here with us, even though he has total control of her actions. It's the temporary release Shana had to fight to achieve the moment she told me to wake up, but Leanne isn't as strong. She just wants help. She distorts again, and Slender-Leanne is standing less than a foot away from me once more.

"I didn't come here for you," I try, hoping that's the right answer. Leanne does the scariest thing she could possibly do next, she laughs. As she laughs her body distorts- no contorts, violently, as if disjointed, and she keeps flashing between no-face and angry-face, while manically laughing, but her laugh is coming from all directions. I feel a sudden drop in my sanity and consider running, but where?

Leanne grabs my head and my shoulder and pulls herself forward as if she were trying to kiss or head-butt me. As her face connects with mine, there's no impact, instead it feels like we are merging, and a deafening static shriek permeates the air. I feel the same vertigo and sudden weakness I experienced the last time. I pull away and catch a glimpse of what's happening.

My light is dimming and it's as if- Leanne is creating the same effect that the tree's vortex did before. Only this time it feels like my whole body is being sucked in by the contact. My body distorts now, painfully. I jump back, and pull away as fast as I can, but Leanne won't relent. I see light coming from her body now. She's stealing my own energy from me! I jerk to my right and run, but my guitar strap pulls me back. I turn my neck and see she's trying to hold onto me by my guitar. She pulls back as I pull forward.

In my current condition- dizziness, numbness, and nausea, I am in no shape to fight her back, and I hit the ground, but before she can grab me and finish me off, I slip under the guitar strap and bolt. Bolt may not be the best word for it. I am practically throwing myself from tree to tree, unable to balance for more than a few steps without falling over, at least not until the dizziness subsides. I can hear Leanne's overwhelming laughter continue, and I turn to see she's following me. She's taunting me. As my vision returns- somewhat, I can run more steadily. I run for maybe twenty seconds before a hand makes contact with my face.

It's Jason's hand. I flinch, ready to be knocked back by the solid force of a punch, and although I fall over, it's not because of any impact. When Jason's hand comes into contact with my face, I feel the same draining sensation. *Does everyone who touches me here steal my life-force?* I wonder.

I push myself up to get off the ground, but Leanne has caught up and her added onslaught worsens my condition. The world is spinning so fast that I can't even see, and it's all I can do to pitch forward, onto my knees, and then try to stand. I hobble between the flashes of pain that come with every distortion, and I feel my light growing even dimmer. When they fully drain me, do I become one of them?

I jerk back and throw a punch at Leanne, but she doesn't react to it. She's just trying to absorb me. I dive away and end up rolling down the hill. The momentum, which I'm grateful for, rips me out of their grip. It's perfect timing too, because there was no way I was getting out of there with my own strength, not when I can't hurt them. I have no weapons here. Without even being able to see clearly, I move on aimlessly. My only desire is to put some distance between my attackers and me.

They siphon my strength like Slender does. They're like variants of him—or maybe extensions of him. My mind starts calling them *Slender Children*. I noticed that they grow brighter as they drain me. Does that mean that if they steal enough from me, they can escape? Is that Slender's game? Whichever one of them takes the most life from me gets released? Or does draining me sufficiently just trap me here?

I just want Adam, and since they drain my energy with contact, do I have to find Adam and give him my strength to help him escape? Shana hadn't drained me this way, so this must just be an attack method. The only way to get out of here is to run. If I fail, then both of us are stuck here. I'll have to take him to the edge like I did Shana and hope he still has enough strength to survive the transition. When I do that will Slender focus on me to make sure I don't escape?

I keep running. I can see one of the girls Deputy Yew showed me a photo of approaching. I turn and run in the opposite direction, only to run into Lindsay. I want to apologize to her, because the first face I see of her is a pleading look on her face, but my judgment tells me to jump away, and I do in the nick of time. As soon as I leap, Lindsay flashes into her faceless form and reaches her arms forward. She wants to drain from me too. It's a game of keep-away.

I dash as fast as I can down through the woods. I need to find Adam, but so far he hasn't appeared. How will I find him?

"Adam!" I try to call, but the static is still distorting my voice.

"Adam!" I scream this time. I'm louder, but I doubt anyone more than five meters away would be able to hear me. A child catches my attention to my left. I stop and lean against the nearest tree to keep from falling over.

"Adam?" I ask, but it's too dim to see from this distance. I hear the laughter of Lindsay, Leanne, Jason, and a few others behind me. If all of them dog-pile me, I'm finished.

I walk forward to illuminate the child, but stop as he comes into view. It's Lionel, faceless Lionel. He distorts and becomes crying Lionel. I wish I'd looked away. I wish I'd turned as soon as I saw that it isn't Adam. The face of a five year old child in pain, full of terror, trauma, and anguish will never leave me. I fight back tears as I run, knowing that Slender did that on purpose, and that Lionel will only grab me like the others. I came here to save Adam, my brother, and if anyone is going to siphon my life from me to escape, it will be him.

"Adam!" I call repeatedly. My voice is getting tired, but weariness isn't an excuse. I bet I haven't been here ten minutes, and I'm sure as hell not going to let being out of breath stop me from rescuing Adam this quickly. Now is not the time for tears. It's not time to break down and admit defeat. "No time to cry," I tell myself, as the song pops into my head.

"Adam!" I call once more.

I can hear Lionel laughing now. He may be the most helpless, the most innocent of all of the children I've seen Slender take, but his laughter is the most sinister. I'd rather have Chucky chasing after me than a giggling Slender-Lionel. "Just ignore it. Let it go," I tell myself, knowing Lionel wouldn't be doing this to me if he had a choice.

I hear them all laughing as they pursue me, but when I turn I can only see about three meters behind me, and I greatly wish I hadn't let Leanne drain so much of me. I should have run as soon as she laughed, or just ignored her. I've fallen for Slender's traps and now I can't even see if my predators are catching up or not. I see more children, most of whom I don't know by name, but I have seen their faces before. These don't wait for me to approach. They just dart in to intercept me.

Ignoring the creeping numbness, I do my best to sprint, dodging trees and roots that would impede my path. Most of them seem like they will catch up to me at the speed they're running, and their ability to appear suddenly, why aren't they all upon me yet? Realization sets in. I'm being herded.

If I could look around, I might have an idea for where I'm going, but my field of vision is limited. I hear one more voice chime in, and this one makes me stop for a single second to mouth the name. "Adam." He repeats his call.

"Alyssa!" he shouts, very audibly. It came from in front of me, slightly to my right. I follow the sound, shouting his name. When he comes into view he takes off running. Why's he running from me? Oh right, I'm being herded. With my track experience and his broken arm, I should be able to catch up to him easily, but Slender has control of him now, and that's even more obvious when his body warps almost out of my line of sight in a single distortion.

.

I follow Adam, with a choir of laughing Slender-Children behind me, for what feels like ten minutes, before he stops in his tracks. I don't stop- not immediately, and I put a hand on him as soon as I catch up, only to be siphoned at the touch. I jerk away and catch what he's staring at.

My eyes begin to sting before I register what it is. The Slender Man is standing in the middle of the clearing, but this time I don't close my eyes. If I am to meet with the Death incarnate, I am going to look him in the eye. As I stare him down, the stinging turns into a continuous burn. The name "The Slender Man," suits him well, but he's taller than I remember him. This must be his full-length form. He stands maybe fifteen feet tall, and yet thin as I am. He has that imperfect stillness to him, only interrupted by its distortions. It looks like I'm gazing at a shadow, except the shadow has taken a three-dimensional form and is standing over me.

My body is screaming at me to close my eyes, and my neck is involuntarily twitching trying to get me to look away. The Slender Children have all caught up, but they're not in pursuit. They've done their jobs. When their laughter stops as well, I can't tell if they've just quieted, or if they've disappeared, because I am looking at Slender, not his minions.

"I came here," I start, surprised that my voice is coming through clearly despite my proximity to the entity that's caused all of this. "...like you told me to. Now I want Adam," I finish. He doesn't move, but Adam's movements catch my eye and I look down at him. His left arm hangs limp by his side, but with his posture you wouldn't even tell that it's broken. He distorts to face-less Adam, and then to the angry-faced version. He changes back and forth, but not once do I see the crying, weakened, real version of Adam.

He backs up, as if seeking Slender for comfort. My heart skips a beat. I didn't come here for Adam to run from me. Was this Slender's plan all along? I close my eyes to hold back from crying. I won't let his victory be so easy.

"Adam it's me. It's Alyssa," I say. Adam doesn't seem convinced. Slender bends over and I feel that resonating screech. He's laughing at my attempt. I shake my head.

"Adam! Get over here now!" I shout. Adam backs into Slender, and it's as if he is being absorbed into his form.

I watch in horror as Adam practically disappears as Slender contorts in response. After Adam has fully disappeared, a long tendril sticks out from Slender's back. As the tendril unfurls, I can hear Adam screaming, and then more tendrils emerge, each one accompanied by a new scream. I refuse to look away. I have to show him that I'm strong enough to handle him. I've heard enough screams. He'll have to show me something new.

My eyes burn, but I do my best to glare at him, show him my anger through it. "Give me my brother back!" I demand. He laughs again. He shape-shifts and shrinks to about seven feet, but it's not his size that matters, it's the face that appears. I'm looking at Adam, but a black, full shadow version of Adam. Slender is mocking me. He must be enjoying his thought of triumph.

I think about what Bubbe and Mr. Mario said. I have to use joy and life to bring him back, and I bring that with music, but I dropped my guitar back there. Then Bubbe's words ring in my ears, and I begin singing. I sing the song I came here with, Adam's favorite song. I sing Adon Olam. I look Slender right in his imitation of Adam's face as I sing it. I sing it through his laughter and distortions, through his static and the cracks in my voice. I ignore him. I'm singing to Adam. He's the one I want. He's the one I came here for.

I reach the second verse and Slender begins contorting again, and I can hear Adam's sobs. He's not screaming now, he's just crying. I ignore him and sing louder. I'm getting more off-key, but I think it's working. Adam stifles his sobs as if he's listening to me. I realize I closed my eyes during my song. I open them and see Adam, the real Adam, peeking out through Slender.

He's crawling forward, distorting sometimes, but he's not marked by one of Slender's tendrils anymore. *I've brought out the real Adam!* I crack a smile when I see him. It's a smile of temporary relief, but I know the fight isn't over, not yet at least. I don't stop singing though, and I hold my hand out for Adam to grab. He doesn't take it though, he can't. He needs his good hand to balance.

I reach forward and take him in my arms. I immediately feel that Adam is draining my life on contact, but I ignore it. I feel as if I'm slipping through him, but with me being absorbed into him, his body follows me as I rise into an upright position. I let go as he's standing, and look up at Slender. He's waiting, as if pondering his next move, and then he makes it. He shakes wildly and I see his tendrils leave him in the form of his Slender Children. Besides Adam, he has twelve of them, four of them I know: Lindsay, Jason, Leanne, and Lionel. He doesn't have Shana to sic on me, but that's a victory on my part.

"Adam, we have to run," I say, but Adam looks hesitant. Slender hits me with that vortex and I feel my life being drained.

"Adam now!" I take off, dragging Adam behind me. My life-force is draining quickly, but with me pulling Adam along and running away from Slender, I'm hoping that whatever I lose is now actually going into Adam and not to Slender. We can't move quickly, but I don't stop.

The Slender Children keep warping right in front of me, and each time I pass one it lashes at me, stealing an ounce here or there. I keep going. My field of vision is blurry, especially with maintaining contact with Adam, and every minute my light grows dimmer. I stick my right hand out and each time it hits a tree I work my way around it. Adam sometimes lets go and when he does I have a moment of respite, but my vision doesn't clear and I'm more worried about losing track of him than not being able to see. Luckily he's glowing more brightly than I am so it makes him easy to find. My hands and feet are guiding me in the shadow world now.

We're going uphill now, and I dry-heave from the effort. I do it on the move though; I have to keep moving, because every few seconds another one of the Slender Children, or maybe Slender himself is striking out at me. I am using what little light I have left, no the light I've given to Adam, to help guide me.

We keep running with the screams and laughs of the children all around us. The vertigo is overwhelming and I find that Adam's hand is now guiding me forward. Adam is leading me now, like I did with Shana, only now I'm the one Slender is feeding on. My feet slip and I'm down on my knees doing the best I can to crawl forward. I don't have much energy left. "Adam, keep running," I say weakly. He let's go.

"I can't. Alyssa, I can't," he cries.

"Leave me, just run," I say, trying to rise back up. I anticipate a mass of hands feeding on me, draining my last legs as I struggle to move forward. What if they feed on Adam too? "Adam, you have to run!" I shout as loudly as I can, which is barely above a whisper.

"I can't, Alyssa. They're everywhere," he says. With no physical contact with Adam, my vision has begun to return. I climb up, and with the few meters of light radiating from his aura, I see where we are. A helpless cry escapes when I see that the Slender Children have us surrounded and are closing in slowly, circling their prey. I walk forward a few paces trying to find an out, but hopelessness consumes me as my knees buckle once more. I sit here one knee on the ground and one leg trying to push me back up, waiting to be consumed. *It's over. I've lost.* There's no- there's a gap. It's only a couple meters wide, but- I feel a meager bit of hope hit me. If I can make it through I might be able to leave them behind, at least until they warp again. It's time to make a last stand.

"Let's go," I say.

"We have to run past them," I continue. It's a last ditch resort, but it's the only way I have left.

"They'll catch us," Adam protests, but I laugh.

"Guess this is where I die," I say, although I'm not even sure if Adam will make it even if I get him through. I rise quickly, my body being powered by a final surge of energy. It's just enough, just enough to get by them. I lift Adam onto my back ignoring the pain as his body drains me. My last bit of strength- my last will is to keep my brother safe. I put a foot forward and take off. The Slender Children go from their slow prowling to trained sprinters inside of a- distortion. I feel hands on me, hands that are not Adams, but I ignore them. The only way to get them off is to move. I run right through one of them. I can't see anything, and the painful experience of such a collision nearly stops me right there, but I give myself every mental reassurance that I can win this. *Just ten more paces… ten more seconds. We're almost there,* I tell myself.

I keep going, my feet hitting the ground so heavily that my steps seem to displace the black earth beneath me. I feel like I'm running faster than I ever have before, even in the real world. Even with Adam latched onto me like a parasite as he unwillingly feeds on my life-force. I can't tell if the numbness is helping me or hindering me, but I'm pretty sure if I could actually feel what I was doing, I wouldn't be able to do it. I must have dashed fifty meters, but every few steps an unwanted hand touches me, siphoning my last remaining bits of energy. They're on my thighs, shoulders, arms, and even my head. Are they running with me, warping in front of me, or do they just have really long arms? I can't see. I can't see a thing in front of me now. It's not worth thinking about. I can't think. I don't have any strength to think.

I take another step, but I don't reach ground immediately, and my heart skips a beat. "Downhill…" I say aloud, almost chuckling. I try to recover by throwing my next leg forward to catch myself, but it's too late. I feel my knee hit the ground, followed by my chest and then onto my side. I am thankful for the numbness now. I can't feel any pain as my body slams into the ground during my tumble. I'm falling down. My brain is shutting down. I catch a glimpse of something in the split second before I hit it. It's a large tree. *Thud.*

"Ah...ugh," I groan.

I roll over but my back is against something. I feel wet, and everything is bright. I cough weakly. "Am I dead?" I ask aloud. I feel something pushing me.

"Alyssa," a distorted voice calls.

"Alyssa, wake up. Don't be dead!" it shouts. I still hear static, but it's more broken than before. I can see a little bit more. I can see branches. The person speaks again. "Alyssa!"

"Adam," I groan. My vision returns a little bit, but it keeps going blurry again. I'm in the forest, and Adam is leaning over me, trying to rouse me with his good arm. I look him in the eye. He looks normal aside from paleness and a few bruises. I cough again and try to move. My body is still very numb, and it's another few seconds before I can so much as hug Adam. I look at my body to identify the wetness, and realize that it's not broken static that I hear.

"Rain," I grunt. It hurts to talk. I try and get up, but it's still a while longer before I can roll over onto my stomach. Now I have to push myself up.

I slowly make it to my feet and Adam helps me stand the rest of the way up. My vision is still blurry, but I can see Adam coated in muddy leaves. I lean forward- nearly falling on him, and kiss him on the top of his head.

"We did it?" I ask. I look around. It's morning and I see no sign of the Slender Man, although I feel like moving around is still as difficult, and now that the numbness has dispersed some more, I realize I'm banged up pretty bad from the fall. My vision clears up a bit and I look around. I think I can make out the trail about ten meters away.

"Come on," I mumble to Adam, still feeling weak. "You okay?" I ask, finding that I have a small limp. A lot of my pain seems to throb from my thigh and back, but the most intense is coming from my head. I must have hit it, but at least feeling is returning to me

The Slender Man

"Where's the bus?" asks Adam.

"Bus?" I ask, not sure what he's talking about. "We need an ambulance," I mutter. He follows me and we find out that it was the trail I saw. We follow the trail towards the school. We aren't too deep into the woods, so it'll only be a bit longer before I can- "Ugh," my vision blurs again and I stumble. "I think," I huff. "I think I hit my head, a little too hard," I say through short breaths.

"Where's Denise? We need to find her!" he protests. What is he talking about? Denise, she's dead right?

"Adam, Denise isn't here," I say, trudging along. I can see the road just ahead. For the millionth time I anticipate Slender stealing me away at the last moment. *Slender!* Something is wrong. This escape was suspiciously easy. Why has he stopped pursuit? I fell down hill and was knocked out, and now I'm back? He wanted me. I was the one who escaped, stealing one of his children and now I've done it again? That doesn't sit right. He'll be back.

"No, she was sitting right beside me," he protests, tugging. My train of thought returns to him. He's talking about Denise.

"No just, we need police," I mutter. We make it through the edge of the woods safely, but my vision blurs again. I try shaking my head to clear things up but it only makes it worse. I pull Adam along the road, hoping someone will be out driving this early. After another minute I see a car in the distance and wave. The car is coming in our direction. I rush forward, pulling Adam with me as fast as I can, with a minor limp. I almost think we aren't going to make it. Maybe we aren't as visible in this rain, but then I realize that it's driving slowly, as if the driver is scanning the woods already. As I get closer I see that it's a police car and it's already come to a halt by the time I register who's driving it.

"Oh my god!" I hear Deputy Yew shout. "Alyssa, you found him! Oh-" he rushes over to us. "Are you alright?" he asks when he gets close.

"Uh, I think I need… ugh," I start. I see his flashlight light, but I can't tell what direction he pulled it out from.

"Follow the light for me." I try to, but my vision blurs.

"Were you attacked or…?"

"I was running and- I fell…" I answer.

"Running? From…"

"I'll explain later, but… but yeah," I say. I can't seem to form full length sentences.

"I think you might have a small concussion, here come with me. We'll get you to some medical attention," he instructs. He puts Adam and me in the back seat. I'm on the driver's side and I lean against the window. I notice I've tracked a lot of mud into the car, and the rainwater is ebbing into the seats. I feel a little sorry because Deputy Yew will probably be the one to clean it up. I hold Adam's shoulder since his left arm is broken. He's holding his left arm, wincing.

"I hurt my arm," he says.

"Adam that's been, that's... you'll be fine," I say.

"What about Denise and the others? They're still at the bus?" he asks.

"Adam, that accident..." I try, but I give up. It's not worth the energy to speak. I lean against the headrest and let out a little laugh. We both made it! We both escaped, for now at least. I thought he wanted me to stay in exchange for Adam though. I thought he wanted *me* for certain.

Deputy Yew is on his radio. "...Yes that's correct. I have *both* of the Redwood children. Alyssa found the boy," he explains. I look through the front window but my vision blurs again, damn concussion.

As my vision returns I see something far ahead in the road. It looks like a person and I brace myself for Deputy Yew to slam the brakes and slam my already weakened body forward. Even with a seatbelt I'm not- he's not slowing down, and I get a closer look. *It's him!* It's The Slender Man in the middle of the road! As the car speeds closer I see him raise one of his hands out as if reaching for me. There's an immense wave of static.

"Look out!" I scream, but it's too late, the car crashes into the Slender Man and I watch his hand reach right through Deputy Yew and right into my face. The only thing I hear over my own scream is Slender's laughter.

Epilogue:

Deputy Terrence Yew abruptly lost radio contact with the sheriff's station while reporting that he had recovered Alyssa and Adam Redwood. A squad car was sent immediately to the deputy's last known location. The responding officer/deputy reported that the deputy was dead, but Adam Redwood was alive and in the car. He had crashed into an unknown object that was at first speculated to be a hit-and-run, but collision reports indicate that the front of the car was deeply dented into a V-shape by an object that was something too slender to be any type of automobile.

The damage from the crash doesn't appear to have been what killed the deputy. There was a large wound through the deputy's chest that ran all the way through his seat that suggests that he was impaled. When Adam Redwood was questioned, he didn't seem to recall anything that happened after a recent bus accident that claimed the lives of several children.

A search party was sent into the forest to find more information about the crash and to search for Alyssa Redwood. Her guitar was found muddied but intact in a pile of leaves. A small distance away from the guitar, a few members of the search party noted that one of an odd tree's lower branches had a large amount of blood on it and around that branch was a large copper Star of David necklace that the Redwood family confirmed had been in the possession of Alyssa Redwood the last time she'd been seen...

DNA analysis of the blood sample taken from the branch revealed that it belonged to Deputy Yew. The bark on the trunk of the tree was severely gouged, and had paint marks that matched the paint of Deputy Yew's patrol car, and microscopic bits of glass taken from the tree branch matched the glass from the windshield. The diameter and shape of the tree exactly matched the indention in the front of the car, indicating that the tree was what the patrol car had collided with, however the vehicle was found more than two miles from the tree and there were no tire marks in the leaves and mud, damage to trees between the damaged tree and the road, or other evidence that the vehicle had veered into the forest. No other signs of Alyssa Redwood were ever found.

Concept Art Section:

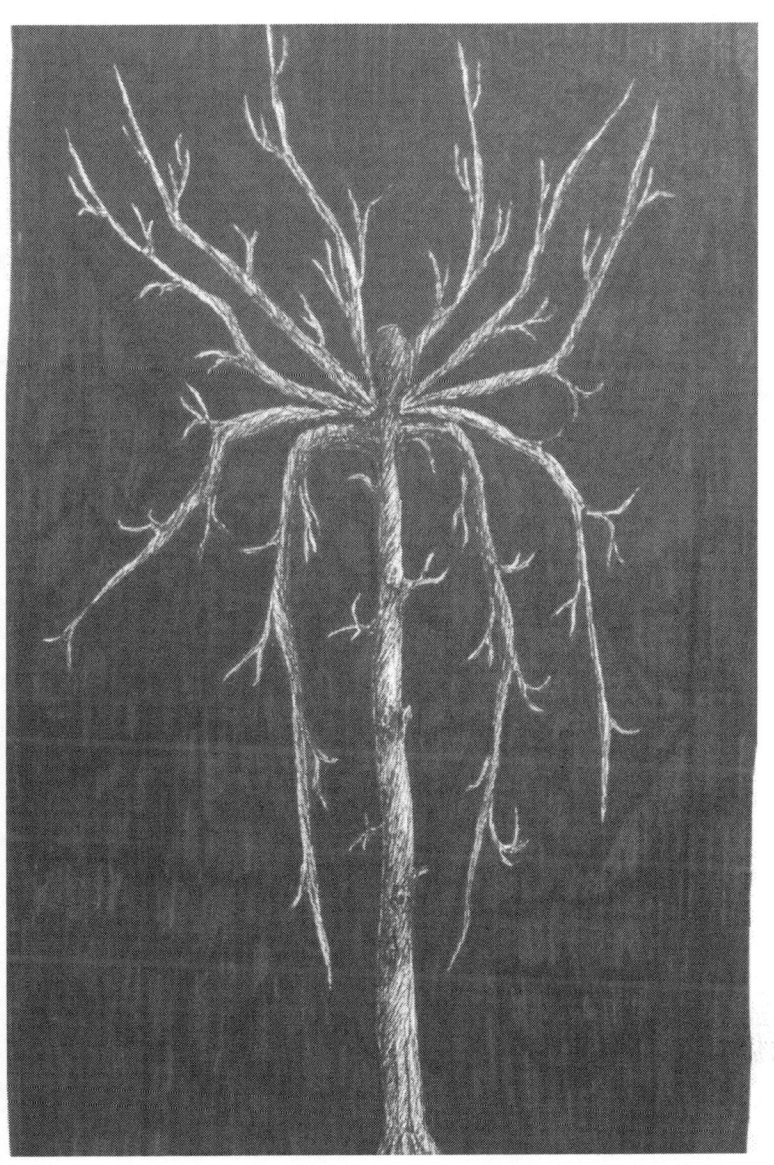

About the Author:

Dexter Morgenstern was born in North Carolina and has been home-schooled most of his life in part due to being diagnosed with Asperger's Syndrome at an early age, which led to being somewhat socially outcast. Over time, Dexter developed a vivid imagination and love for chemistry and biology. This led him to delve into the world of science fiction and begin writing at the age of fifteen.Dexter combined his imagination with his appreciation for science, and competed in the NaNoWriMo contest in 2011 at the age of 17. He successfully finished the contest and finally drafted his first novel, *Felix Faust* as part of the Arcane Insurrection series.

Visit him at http://DexterMorgenstern.com

About the Artist:

Anna is a Swedish artist and art teacher who recently moved to Washington State. She has a background within the art and media field from several art schools and universities and received her MA in 2010. Anna's artwork mainly contains mixed media where graphical drawings and sculpture are the two main elements. She has a great interest in fantasy worlds and gathers her inspiration from the deep forests of nature, old folklore stories and things unexplained.

Printed in Germany
by Amazon Distribution
GmbH, Leipzig